Black

A Novel by S. R. Case

xulon
PRESS

For my dear friends,
the students and teachers of the Toastmasters Youth
Program,
who were my satisfied test-subjects.

Chapter 1

B lack. That simple name alone does the color no justice. What I saw when I opened my eyes wasn't just black, it was a deep and empty pit of nothing that was to become my world.

For some reason, my one thought was that my eyes were open - I should be seeing something. I couldn't see a thing, and I couldn't hear, either. *Why aren't my eyes working?* I thought. *Why aren't my ears working?* I don't know how long I lay like that, confused.

No word can describe the piercing, screaming noise that seared into my brain and made me cover my ears. At least my hands were working, and after a while I figured out my ears were, too. The first noise I actually recognized was a woman crying. She was sobbing, and I couldn't understand what she was saying.

What happened to me?! I was suddenly so unaware of where I was that my brain blurted it out.

Then my brain did what most people call a flashback. When people have flashbacks in movies their past shoots rapidly before their mind's eye. It really does happen. I flashbacked and realized that I had been in an airplane crash. I could hear it going down, hear screaming, could see the plane rip apart. It was terrifying.

What was making it black? A throbbing pain in my head and something trickling down my nose told me I'd been injured. I reached up to my face and knew instinctively blood was gushing out of my forehead.

Now, what was making it black? I stretched my arms above my head but there was nothing above or around me. I reached down to find something grainy below me. It felt like sand. What was I doing on sand? Shouldn't I be in an airplane?

I felt dizzy, and like my stomach was crawling up my throat.

The first thing I thought to do was call for help. Generally, when blood is fountaining from your head and you feel faint, you do that.

I tried. No sound came out. I tried again. It was very scratchy. I tried repeatedly, and by the tenth try I was screaming so loud I was scaring myself.

Then worse black. I had blacked out completely - pun intended. When I came to again, it was still black. I felt something heavy on me, smothering me. The breath was rushing out of my lungs like air out of a leaky balloon. The thing on top of me was soft and warm and killing me and I couldn't push it off. "HELP!" I screamed again.

"Oh my God, there's somebody alive!" a muffled voice yelled.

Of course I'm alive, I thought. *Why shouldn't I be?*

The person's remark reminded me that there was a God, which gave me the thought that praying seemed like a good idea. So I prayed. "Please take away the black." I actually prayed out loud, with what little breath I had. "And let me live."

Something grabbed my ankles and yanked me out from under the heavy thing. "Are you okay?" a British voice said. It was a man. I was suddenly very glad the British were created.

"I'm...okay now." It took a lot of strength to get the words out. "Can you uncover my eyes? I'm going nuts, not seeing anything."

No one answered.

"Are you still there?" I asked impatiently, still gulping in air.

"Y-Yes, I'm here," Mr. British said.

"Well? How about it?" Another minute of silence, in which I had time to think of reasons why I couldn't see. "Oh. Oh, no." I didn't have enough breath to say more. I realized immediately what had happened to me. I was very upset about it, because I was always good at seeing the details in life, as my brother always said.

I was blind.

It's probably worse to see before you go blind, to know what you're missing.

The shock hit me hard and I was speechless. I wasn't sure what to think anymore, and I started shaking with emotion. I felt a strong hand on my shoulder. "Calm yourself," the Brit commanded. He had a deep voice, a rough accent. There was something reassuring about the way he spoke.

I calmed. I didn't mean to cry, but tears were running down my cheeks. "My head," I said, because the blindness problem could be sorted out later – right now my head hurt like crazy.

"You have a very bad gash on your forehead," he told me. I could feel him touching my head, examining it.

"You a doctor?" I asked flatly.

"Yeah, I am. This cut looks pretty bad." He was moving as he talked. "Can you tell me who you are?"

"Oh, no." I had absolutely no idea. Not a single clue. "I was in a plane crash..." I offered.

"Yeah."

"Uhhh...I..." I still had no idea, and I couldn't seem to talk anymore.

The Brit talked. He had a rather reassuring voice. It was nice to listen to. "You've got a nasty head injury, probably caused a concussion as well as the blindness. I'm putting this on the wound to sterilize it." He poured something cold and terrible all over my head. It dripped onto my tongue and I tasted alcohol. I wondered where he got it. Amazing the little things you think about in a crisis.

"And I'm putting this clof over it," he went on. He meant 'cloth.' Most of his 'th's sounded like 'f's. He took my hand and set it on the cloth. "Press down on it. Most of the bleeding has stopped...I can't do anyfing else. We'll move you over somewhere else and take care of you then. Right now..."

"The crash," was all I said. I knew there were people worse off than me, though I couldn't imagine them being too much worse. I didn't hear him go. I was very still for a while.

"Hi." The voice was so awkward I could tell the person was staring at me. Maybe at my eyes. I wondered if they looked any different.

"Hi," I said to the voice, which was a woman. Probably a young woman. Definitely an American.

"I'll stay with you a while...I'm Jane."

"Good." I didn't define what I meant by that. I wasn't thinking clearly enough to define anything at all.

"You really had us worried. We thought you were...a... body. We piled you in with the rest of the bodies and when you yelled..."

"Scared you?"

"Yeah. Still can't remember who you are?"

"No." I had to work on that. And I worked on it for a long time, because the American girl didn't say anything else. She most likely left me. I tried to remember who I was, but I couldn't.

I had a brother. I was in an airplane. I used to be able to see.

I tried to reason out the muddle of my brain, until I was carried somewhere and I fell asleep from exhaustion, laying on something grainy, probably sand.

From the time I woke up blind to the time I was carried away from the pile of bodies was the most confusing, horrendously upsetting moments of my life. Every second of it is stuck in my brain because it was so awful.

When I woke up yet again, my head was still killing me, my stomach was still climbing my windpipe and I still didn't know who I was.

And, I was still blind.

"Hi," a voice said, "it's me, Jane." She had a soft voice.

"Hi," I croaked. How long had she been sitting there?

"Can you remember who you are yet?"

"No." I laid there for a while. I could feel clues to myself floating around the back of my mind. Having an idea, I reached into my pocket, searching for some kind of identification. I dumped the contents onto the ground. "What's in my pocket?"

"Uh, bubble gum…thirty-five cents. That's it."

I sighed. "Help me out here. What do I look like?" It was a strange question to be asking someone, but I had no other clues.

"Well…brown eyes…dark brown hair…it's kind of wavy. Uh…you have nice teeth…" She laughed quietly.

I laughed along. She sounded nice.

"Your skin…kind of pale with yellow undertones…"

I felt my face. Kind of rough. Bumpy near the end of my jaw. "Am I a teenager?" Wow. That was a weird question.

"Yeah, I guess. Can you tell the FBI wouldn't take me?" She was laughing at herself. "Okay, okay, small nose, good solid bone structure…I'd say you were five-foot-six…five-seven? I can't tell when you're laying down."

I could kind of piece myself together. At first I was a blurry mess, and as I toyed with the picture in my mind, it all became clear. My image appeared before my mind's eye, clear and 3-D. She wasn't bad at describing me. I'd say I was five-five and maybe a half but I'd claim five seven if she'd give it to me.

I guess when my brain got my picture everything else fell into place.

"Hey!" I said excitedly to Jane. "I know who I am."

American, my brain was telling me, *fourteen years old (only that old?), my name is Richard Malcolm Ferrell, I was born in Chicago, Illinois, I have an older brother, Noah David Ferrell, a goldfish, and I like Classical music, which is lame of me.* Everything I was supposed to know came next, and my brain was telling me I was back to normal.

Both my parents were dead. They died two years ago in a car accident. I'd been living with my aunt Sandy and her family until four months ago, when my brother Noah came to take me to be with him over the summer.

Aunt Sandy was having a hard time dealing with her kids and needed some space. Noah thought he'd let me tag along with him and his airplanes. So I'd been flying all over the place with him for four months, living on the plane, in hotels, and his upper-class apartment in Chicago sometimes.

Oh, no...my brother.

"What happened to the pilot?" I asked frantically.

"Who? The pilot? Why?"

"He's Noah Ferrell, he's my brother."

"I...I don't know. The airline staff didn't make it. We haven't found the pilot..." Her voice trailed off and I knew what she was thinking.

Please God, I prayed again, don't let him die. I wasn't overly religious, but I knew when prayer counted.

"We'll find him," Jane said. "What's your name?"

"Rick Ferrell. Only don't ever call me Ricky." I had to make that clear right off. I hated 'Ricky', as far as I could remember.

"Sure thing. We'll look for your brother. A bunch of us are going on a hike to scout out the place later on." Something about her voice was reassuring, like the doctor's.

"Hey…where are we?"

"I don't know. We're on a beach…but there are lots of grassy places like meadows beyond here, just behind a tree-line."

"We crashed on a beach?"

"Yeah. Two days ago."

"What?"

"That's why we piled some of the bodies up already. They were everywhere."

That heavy thing that was smothering me must have been a body. *Ugh.*

"How many people died?"

"Out of a hundred passengers…sixty."

"Wow. It was bad, then?"

She must have nodded. "I have to go. I'll be back."

"Okay." I assumed someone had called her. My ears were still ringing so I couldn't hear too well.

I remembered the crash. I wished I hadn't.

Chapter 2

We were coming back from London and heading to LAX. Normally we would have flown over the Atlantic, but there were too many storms. We had flown across the continent with a fuel stop in Hong Kong, and now we were over the Pacific. I was sitting in the jump-seat behind Noah and he was saying something about the radar. Trying to explain it to me, but he was joking about half of it. He was one of those young guys who can't help being funny. He always grinned. He looked like me a little, although he was very tall and a bit on the stocky side. He was good looking, though. Most importantly, he was the best brother ever.

Suddenly we lurched like we'd hit a bump. Noah started talking excitedly to Mick, the co-pilot, in a worried voice, saying something about an unusual amount of air pockets. Mick said something about effects on air currants from the Atlantic storms. Noah flipped on the seatbelts light and the three of us buckled in. He spoke to the passengers about turbulence being normal this time of year. Gwen, the stewardess, poked her head in to see what was wrong.

"Get in your seat!" Noah yelled to her.

I was worried. The plane began shaking like it was in a giant blender. After a few minutes of it, I started praying. It was the only thing I knew to do when hope was fading.

"Rick!" Noah looked at me. "Get in the staff seat." By 'the staff seat' he meant the one that wasn't in the cockpit. He considered it safer, in case of a crash.

"Noah, maybe it's just-"

"Rick. There is something wrong. Just until I get this thing smoothed out."

"Noah-"

"C'mon, buddy, I have enough to worry about with Mick at the controls."

"Hey!" Mick gave a defensive look.

Noah gave me a little push. "C'mon, kid, don't make me put you in that seat. Do it for me." He seemed nonchalant, but when my eyes met his I knew he was worried.

"Fine, fine," I grumbled and unbuckled out of the jump-seat. I left the cabin and strapped into a seat in the first row of staff chairs. I was only supposed to sit there during emergencies. Noah had pulled some strings to let me on the plane, and the staff seat was an extra string pulled.

Gwen strapped in beside me. She glanced over at me and smiled. "Fun, huh?"

"Not really." I was always nervous on flights.

"Rick, you're so cynical. They're steering away from the turbulence. This'll be over in a minute."

I had to trust her. Because I had traveled with her often, and because she was so close to Noah, Gwen had become like my big sister. Besides, she was also usually right about these things.

"Boy," sighed Gwen, "if it's this bad here I can't imagine how rough it is over the Atlantic."

In a few seconds it all seemed over. The seatbelt light went off and my brother's voice came over the speakers. "This is your captain speaking. Sorry about this, folks. There's a lot of turbulence out here. Please remain in your seats 'til I say so. I'm currently maneuvering around the problem area. We'll be in LA at three o'clock p.m."

Gwen un-belted and I saw the passengers start doing the same. She stood up and headed for the cabin.

"Where are you going? He said to stay seated."

"Oh, Rick." *She went in the cabin.*

I remained stubbornly strapped in. After sitting there a while like a fool, I took the seatbelt off.

And then, without warning, we plunged. We took a huge dip and I clung to my chair.

"This is your captain!" *Noah shouted.* "Please get in your seats and buckle up now!"

I did so as we leveled out again. And then I heard the worst sound. An engine exploded. We whipped around and Noah's voice crackled above the screaming. "PLEASE ASSUME CRASH POSITIONS! WE ARE GOING D-" *The rest of it was broken up, but I swear I heard him say my name. We nosed straight down. People who hadn't buckled in yet slid into the wall in front of me and I looked away. The plane groaned and screamed and I heard it rip apart, saw the light stream through the cracks. Oxygen masks fell from the ceiling. As I tried to put a mask on, my seat flipped over and I snapped out of the belt. I felt air rush down my neck and suck at me. I closed my eyes and gasped, unable to breathe. Sickening noises followed, ones I try to forget. Screaming. Crying. Praying. Death.*

I curled into a ball and covered my head. After an eternity of waiting to die, the plane slammed to a stop and slid about a mile as I rolled around and pieces of the plane rained down around me. Something heavy ripped into my scull and I prayed that God would forgive me for my sins. Seemed like a good idea since I was clearly going to die.

"Rick?" Jane was touching my arm. "You alright?"

"Fine." I wasn't fine. I was scared to death for Noah. And Gwen, and Mick, and my airline friends who were all stuck at the front of the plane in those stupid staff seats that broke in half and did no good.

"Rick?" Jane asked again. "You're sweating pretty bad, are you okay?"

"It's hot." I wiped perspiration from my eyes and upper lip and took shuddery breaths. I could feel the sun shining directly on my face.

"Should I get the doctor?"

"No," I sighed. "You don't have to be with me, you know, if you have to do something...I'll be alright."

"It's okay. Right now people are getting set for the hike and there isn't much to do."

"Oh." I tried to think of a conversation starter. "I was wondering..."

"Uh-huh?"

"How it is that the doctor always survives the disaster in some miraculous way?" I was trying to ease the pressure off of myself. I was attempting a sort of joke, but maybe it was working and maybe it wasn't.

"Well...Colin isn't actually a doctor."

"Oh. I thought he said he was."

"Apparently he's still training to be one. That's what I heard."

"Like an intern?"

"Yeah."

"Huh. How old is he?" I was talking to keep her from being bored, but in truth I wanted to go to sleep.

"I don't know." She sounded surprised I'd asked. "Twenty-five...thirty? Again, I'm awful at describing people."

"How old are you?" I asked, curious.

There was a small pause. "Twenty-five. Are you..."

Oh, great. "Hitting on you? No. You're kinda out of my league, and now is not great timing. You just remind me of a friend of mine." I was thinking of Gwen.

"Good. 'Cause you kind of look like my little brother."

Ouch. Maybe I'd better shut up. But my mouth kept running. "You know Colin personally?"

"No. We were sitting next to each other on the plane. I didn't even know his name until we crashed."

"Hmmm…"

"You really don't look good."

"Thanks."

"No, I mean, maybe I should get the doctor."

"Mean the intern?" When she didn't answer I assumed she'd left. It was practically impossible for me to hear anyone walking because of the sand, and I couldn't hear much else because of the waves and the ringing noise in my head.

"Rick?" Jane was back. "I brought Colin, the doctor."

"Intern," I corrected, and actually giggled. *What are you doing?* My brain asked incredulously. You must be *delirious!*

"Rick, can you hear me?" Colin, the Brit, asked.

"Loud and clear," I said wearily. I could feel myself slipping out of reality.

"Let's get 'im out of the sun," Colin commanded, and grabbed my legs.

Jane reached under my arms. "It's alright, Rick. Stay with us." As she leaned over me I smelled Lilly of the Valley.

I landed on some bumpy terrain and heard the rustle of trees.

"You still here?" asked Jane, and she sounded concerned. She sounded like she was talking to her little brother.

I felt hands on my head. Colin swore. "It's infected," he said gruffly, and I assumed he meant the hole in my head.

I could hear Jane breathing. "Hey, Jane…" I started, and threw up. Twice in a row. "Sorry," I sputtered in between.

Colin held me up. "It's okay, it's okay. You're getting the poisons out. Your body's going through a healing process."

It felt more like I was getting worse. "Wish there was an easier way."

Apparently there wasn't an easier way. For two more days I had a fever and threw up a few times, and various people whom Colin assigned to me poured water down my throat to keep me from dehydrating. They also gave me a little food for strength. I knew my caregivers vaguely as Rita, Paul, and a very grumpy old guy, Kurt.

One of the hardest parts was going to the bathroom. Or rather, not having a bathroom to use. People used a spot in the forest where, I was told, there was a thick line of trees, like a screen. I couldn't go when Rita was watching me, because I needed someone to stand close by in case I fell over or something. I had never felt such humiliation as not being able to use the john on my own.

In that time of recovery, I actually started feeling less dizzy but more sick. I was aware of my surroundings, much as I could be without seeing them. It made my being sick more awful.

I was still blind. I kept hoping it would go away, but I knew deep down this was a permanent thing. Colin tried to explain about how when my optic nerve must have been damaged, but I didn't care how it happened. I just knew I was blind. I cried sometimes, when I figured no one was around. I don't know why I cried. Being blind wasn't bothering me as badly as I'd feared. Then again, I knew when I got off this beach and back to the real world the frustration would kick in.

Waiting for help to come, to be rescued, was on everybody's mind. I could hear people bicker over what the priorities were in a situation like this. With each passing day, it became evident the priority was finding more drinking water. Apparently the scouting party Jane told me about had been sent to determine whether there was a water source nearby, and whether there was a shelter in case of storms.

Day Four, hunting was suggested. Food was running thin.

I was content to just sit and wait for a rescue plane. Although I was hungry, I wouldn't keep food down for long. Other people, who didn't have to focus their attention on an injured head, blindness, puking and the like, not to mention wondering where and how their brother was, were restless and bored.

I judged, by remembering all the screens Noah showed me before we hit turbulence, that we were somewhere in the Pacific. The turbulence probably threw us off course. We were like a needle in a big blue haystack. Whoever was looking for us, I realized grimly, was going to look in the wrong place. I was, if possible, more scared than ever.

I asked multiple times where Jane was, and Paul (a young guy, I figured by the way he talked) told me she'd gone off with the scouting party.

On this day, Paul was in charge of me again. Today he was more talkative than usual. I asked him to describe the island for me (assuming it was an island) because I kind of wanted to know where I was, and again, I was trying to keep a fellow passenger from being bored.

"Sure," said Paul obligingly. "There's a huge ocean in front of us."

"Really?" It dripped with sarcasm, and I was sorry immediately. I was too touchy these days.

"Yeah…" Was he offended? "Anyway, like, there's this huge bunch of sand, like a strip, and some of the girls are sunbathing."

"What?"

"Crazy, I know. But I don't really blame 'em. What else are they s'posed to do? Paint their toenails? The tail and midsection of the plane are kinda scrunched up over to your right. Way over farther right is the front of the plane. Between you and that, we've built a few campfires. Beyond all that, there are some major big cliffs. Also to your left, by the trees, we set up a medic tent out of some tarps. There are some seriously injured people in there. Over to your left it just goes on and on and then kinda dips inward. There's, like, open fields behind the trees."

"Thanks."

"Sure."

"What do you look like?"

"Light brown hair, blue eyes, I got the stubble thing goin', but only 'cause I don't have a razor anymore." He was much better at description than Jane.

"Are you tall?"

"Average. I'm a regular dude."

"How old are you?"

"Twenty-two."

"You in a band?"

"Yeah. We're just a garage band. How'd you guess?"

"Shot in the dark."

"I play guitar, piano, violin, sing. My band is called 'Hector.'"

"Why?"

"I don't know. It was cool. I think Hector was a warrior or something…"

"Yeah. He was a prince of Troy."

"Way nerdy, dude. But neat."

"Why were you in London?"

"Oh. My job. I'm a computer salesman and I was sent to a big buyer in London to sell some laptops."

"You must be good at what you do."

"Thanks. I'm trying to make Salesman of the Year. Want my card?"

"Uh…wouldn't do me much good."

"Sorry. I used to have some Braille cards, to give to our customers who bought Braille keyboards."

"I can't read Braille...yet..." A sudden wave of sadness swept over me again. Life would be so strange when I got back home. Where would I live? Would Noah keep me or would I go back to Aunt Sandy?

Noah. I'd have given anything to have him with me. I had no idea where he was, and I missed him so much it hurt.

"How much do you like me, bro?" he'd ask, and I'd say *"Plenty."* And he'd ask if I liked him enough to do something for him. And I'd say yes and end up taking out the trash or washing the dishes or something.

I liked him plenty right now. I wished I'd never left the cockpit. Maybe I'd be with him now, wherever he was.

"You okay, man?" Paul asked, and I realized I'd spaced out on him.

"Fine," I said. "Hey, out of curiosity, would you say I'm five foot seven?"

"Totally," he said. I decided I liked him on the spot. "You look pale. Sure you're fine?"

"Uh-huh. I'm always pale." For all her observation faults, Jane had got my skin color correct: sallow.

"Maybe you should go lay out there with Barbie and Co. and catch some rays," Paul suggested.

"No thanks."

"You want me to describe them for you, too?" I knew he was joking, and it sounded like something Noah would have said.

"No," I said with a short laugh. Then I threw up for the last time.

Later in the afternoon, the scouting party returned. Paul told me they had come back.

"I want to go see what they're saying," I said.

"You shouldn't move, man."

"Please," I went on stubbornly, "I'm feeling better." I wasn't lying. My stomach had quit sloshing so much.

"Alright." He grabbed under my armpits and helped me stand. "Dude, you're a heavy kid."

"Thank you," I panted.

It was maddening, not seeing where I was going. We halted and lurched forward. My nerves told me I was going to run into somebody, something. My feet were clumsy.

All the frustration hit me at once and I collapsed not five feet from where we began.

"You okay, man?" Paul wheezed.

"No!" I shouted, "I am not okay!"

"Still sick?"

"No! It's not being sick, it's because I can't see!" I was really angry now. Why did this happen to me? I had been focused on the pain and sickness before, but now I had to face being blind.

I had to face the blackness.

"Dude, lemme get you some water."

"No," I waved him off. "Just let me sit a minute." I was past crying for myself. I was at an utter boiling point. It's not FAIR! my brain screamed.

I would never, ever see anything again. I'd never wake up and open my eyes and see where I was, what I looked like, what the people I cared about looked like.

I could feel the sun on my face but I couldn't see it shining. I could hear Paul breathing but I couldn't see his face. I could hear people talking, but I had no idea where they were.

"Dude…" Paul said slowly.

"I'm sorry," I sighed heavily, "I'm sorry. Go on. I'm just going to sit here. Go see if they found Noah yet."

"Your brother?"

"Yeah." I had told him about Noah.

"Be right back."

I strained my ears and heard his footfalls in the sand. But I couldn't see him run.

I shuddered. I was mad, but I was scared, too. I was so unsure of everything. Would my life be completely different from now on? Yeah, idiot, I told myself. You're blind.

I could probably handle it. I handled Mom and Dad's death without going nuts on the world. Maybe I could handle not seeing.

My hands were shaking. The anger had gone away, and fear took its place. I was so vulnerable now, like a newborn kitten. Somebody could step on me and squash me and I'd never see it coming. The world was a like a big, black ocean and I couldn't swim well.

Too many analogies…I decided to stick with the ocean. The kitten was too grim a picture.

Maybe if Noah could help me get through the first bit of it I could carry on okay from there. Probably. It wasn't like my life was so complicated. I was one of those background kids that nobody noticed anyway. I knew how to read people because I was always watching them from the sidelines.

"You always see the details in life," Noah said constantly.

"Rick?" I was surprised to hear Jane's friendly voice. "Hi. Paul sent me over here."

"Hi." I felt a little better, having her there. "You know Paul?"

"Not really. How's it going?" she asked slowly.

"Fine." This time I was lying. "Did you find any trace of Noah?"

I heard her shift around. "Uhhmm…Rick…"

"Didn't find him, huh? That's okay. We'll keep looking." *Well, they'll keep looking. I'll sit here and worry.* "Don't feel bad. Noah was always the sneaky type." I acted indifferent, but I was concerned he wasn't anywhere around here. Was he hurt?

Silence.

"Jane, I can't see you," I said harshly. "You're going to have to say something."

"Rick, I'm so sorry." Was she crying? "He was…he must have been thrown from the plane…we found his body way out there in the forest…"

"Oh, God…" My world, what little of it I'd held together, just fell apart. "Are you sure it was the pilot?" I choked.

"Yes. He had his ID. Noah Ferrell."

"Oh, God." I wasn't being blasphemous, I was praying I wouldn't die of shock and depression. I stood up. I held my head and pulled at my hair and started breathing rapidly. I'd always wondered what it would be like to hyperventilate. Now I knew.

Jane grabbed my arm. "Rick, Rick, sit down."

I pulled away. I tried gasping some sort of sentence to swear at the world, to tell Fate how much I hated it, to ask God why he was doing this to me. But I couldn't breathe. So many things that weren't supposed to happen to my body had happened, and it had taken a toll on my sanity. I managed to kick the ground and fall to my knees.

Jane grabbed my face and tried to calm me down. "Please listen to me. It's going to be okay."

"It-is-NOT!" I managed. "It is not-o-kay. *I* am not-o-kay! I can't-even-talk! You-stop-talking!"

Jane got so close I felt her spit landing on me. "You're alive!" she shouted firmly, and took on a voice and apparently an attitude I didn't know she possessed. "Your heart is beating, your limbs are in place and you are talking to me. Do you know how lucky you are? People died and are still dying! Yeah, you can't see now, and you lost the person you loved the most, and it hurts, but you're still here and you're going to be okay!"

I was so amazed at her I started breathing normally again. I had pictured her as kind of a ditzy wimp. That picture went into the mental recycling bin. What was eating her? Whatever it was, it brought me around. Unfortunately, she had a point. "Sorry," I whimpered.

She let go of my face. "Yeah..." she said in a shuddery voice. "Well, it calmed you down." I heard her crunch off through the sand.

Hey, God? Thank you for strong women.

I was devastated, but far from gone. Noah was dead. I was stuck in a scary, dark world where weird American girls wearing Lilly of the Valley perfume could frighten me into my senses.

But I was alive. I guess I'd have to make the best of it.

Chapter 3

I spent the rest of Day Four grieving for Noah and recovering from my injuries and sickness.

Noah was a wonderful brother, and my best friend. He didn't deserve the death he got, though I comforted myself with the fancy that it had been a quick death. He loved me, and had tried to take care of me, although I had probably been a kind of drag on his world-traveling lifestyle. Not many young guys with exciting lives would agree to tote their boring little brother along, but he had. He appreciated family. That's why he liked Gwen.

Poor Gwen. Jane had said the staff didn't make it. And if Gwen was still alive, I reckoned she would have sought me out by now. I should have asked whether Jane had definitely found her body; but Gwen, though she was pretty, might be hard to distinguish between Brandy and Vicky and all the other stewardesses. They looked mostly the same.

I was glad Noah picked Gwen as his favorite, though. She was a bit more down-to-earth than the rest. I knew Noah and she loved each other, and at first I was skeptical of her, but I was actually happy when Noah said he was going to marry her. He proposed to her in London. She had said yes, of course, and they were going to settle wedding plans when we got back to LA. They were inseparable, and that's what had made Gwen go back into the cockpit before the crash.

Now they were gone, at least I was sure Noah was, and here I was, stuck in the middle of the Pacific, feeling sorry for myself.

Colin came by later in the day and said the gash on my forehead was closing up alright now, though he had been worried for a while. The constant fluids he ordered me to take had prevented any dehydration. Now I was just going to have to get used to being blind. Like it was that simple.

He told me some of the passengers' luggage had fallen out of the plane, but they couldn't find mine.

Rita, a nice motherly lady, said the scouting party had found some caves about three miles from the beach. They'd also found a spring with drinking water, but not much to eat.

The day wore on.

Night came slowly. I could tell it was night because the temperature dropped and I couldn't feel the sun shining. I did hear crickets and campfires, which were further clues, and this night I heard someone singing. I was feeling surprisingly better in regards to my health, although I was starving.

Loneliness set in after a few hours and I thought I'd go to sleep. I was still heaped over next to the trees, away from everyone. I had just dropped off when I heard a birdcall. It woke me up and I was turning over on my side when I heard the weirdest noise. It was somewhere between singing and wailing, a sound that sent chills up my spine and reminded me of the horror movies Noah and I used to watch. I sat bolt upright and tried to distinguish where it was coming from. I'd thought at first it was the person I'd heard singing before, but this noise was coming from behind me, through the trees, not from where the rest of the passengers were.

There it went again. I couldn't tell if it was a man or woman. It sounded like it was a long way away. I heard the passengers murmuring. They sounded like they were walking in my direction.

The 'song' accelerated into a louder, high-pitched trill and it was freaking me out. Then it stopped and a very low hum began. I wondered whether, if I could see anything, there would be some sign as to what in the world was going on. We could have been invaded by aliens and I might not know.

I heard somebody come up behind me. "You'd think it was the Twilight Zone," a British man's voice said, but it wasn't Colin's. This accent was more of the cut glass type.

"Yeah," I responded, assuming the guy was talking to me.

"Where's a rescue squad when you need one?" he said through his teeth.

I also wished the cavalry would hurry up and get here. I'd had about enough of this place. "Can you see anything?" I asked.

"I can see as much as you can."

"I doubt that."

"Hey, are you that blind kid?"

"Am I famous?"

He didn't answer that. "All I can see is a bunch of scared people looking at the trees because if whatever's out there is man-eating, we have nowhere to go but the sea."

I hadn't pictured the Voices out there to be anything but human, but now that he mentioned it, it might have been some kind of animal. "If it is man-eating, I'll be the first thing it catches."

Suddenly, I heard an explosion. It rocked the ground and my teeth rattled. I dropped to the sand instinctively. "What was that?" I yelled at the British guy.

"Armageddon." He swore.

"What was it really?"

"Fireworks," he said in amazement. His voice was muffled, and I assumed he was lying in the sand as well.

"Are you serious?" I asked incredulously.

"Yes!"

The weird song swelled into a screeching chorus and then died. All I heard were crickets again.

"Well, what was that all about?" I asked shakily.

"Right."

I sat up. "The Martians have landed," I said in a radio voice. It wasn't exactly funny.

The guy laughed bitterly and I heard him rise and brush his clothes. "You scared yet?"

"Yep." More scared than I could say. Whatever just happened was unnatural. "Will you do me a favor?"

"What?"

"Guide me over to where the other people are. I want to see…hear what they're saying."

He didn't answer, and he was obviously annoyed, but I didn't back out. We stumbled over to the others, and the guy walked away. I hoped I was inconspicuous.

"We have to find the radio and contact help," someone was saying.

"The front part of the plane is smashed in. We'll have to figure out how to get in there." I recognized Colin's voice.

"Great," said someone else. "Whatever it takes."

"When we do find it," Colin continued, "who'll know how to work the radio?"

There were a few hems and haws. Then, "Him." It was Jane who said it. I wondered who the lucky guy was. Silence again. Someone nudged me. "You, kid."

"What?" And then I realized I did know how to work the radio, but that it didn't matter. It probably wouldn't work, if the plane was in as bad a shape as they said it was. The transmitter, however, was what we wanted. It was like a satellite phone. Noah had showed it to me and gave me explicit instructions on how to use it. Fortunately, I was good with electronics. "Sure, I can work the transmitter."

"Transmitter?" someone asked.

"Yeah, well, the actual radio's probably dead," I explained. "But the transmitter is for emergencies."

"He can't do it," somebody said after a minute, and I recognized the voice of the British guy who had brought me over here. "He's blind."

Too true, I thought. "But I can explain to someone else how to use it."

There was a little confusion of voices, then the first voice, an American man, said, "Okay, we'll get the kid to work it."

I was suddenly aware that about forty people were staring at me. I shrunk into myself.

"What about food?" someone asked.

"What about it?" the American voice said. "Tomorrow, after we use the transmitter, we'll be out of here in no time."

"But we should still try and find more food in case," Colin pointed out. "Some of us should look for food while the rest of us find the transmitter. It could still be a while before we get out of here."

"Why?" the American challenged. "Once they get the signal, we can tell them where we are."

"Do you know where we are, Grant?" Colin asked the American. When there was no answer, he said "Rick?"

"Yeah?" So much for being inconspicuous.

"Where are we?"

"I don't know. We were off course when we crashed."

"So how do we let the rescue team know where we are?"

"When we transmit a message, they can follow the signal."

"See?" said Grant. "Simple as that."

"Actually..." I faltered. It was hard to talk in a large group, because I didn't know if someone else was going to speak and I would be interrupting them. I couldn't read their body language. "We have to be able to connect with some-body – a ship or something. Then they have to actually pick up the signal and hold it long enough to track it."

"So what are our chances?" asked Colin.

I considered the question. In reality, there were no definite odds. But forty airplane crash survivors where looking for hope. And, they were all looking to me for it. If I lied and said it was easy, they'd blame me for letting them down if we couldn't get it to work. If I told them the truth, their morale could plummet and they'd still blame me if we couldn't get it to work. Why couldn't someone else know all this transmitter stuff?

"It should be simple," I said, picking Option One. "We only have to transmit for a long period of time, and it's more than likely they'll pick up the signal."

"You're lying," said another voice quietly. I wished I could see who was calling me out.

"Who are you?" asked Grant.

"I'm Professor Taylor," said the quiet voice. "I teach chemistry. I know about radio transmissions though, enough to know that the chances of someone picking up our signal and holding it long enough are slim."

"Why didn't you speak up before when we asked who could work the transmitter?" asked Colin.

"I only understand the science of it."

"But you could make it work."

"Anyone could make it work," countered the professor, "once given basic instructions."

"Is this important?" asked Jane.

"No," answered Grant. "Let's get some sleep. We can't do anything tonight."

Murmuring, the group broke up. Apparently Colin, Grant, Jane, and my British 'friend' with the cut-glass accent stayed behind.

"This could be dangerous, going into the airplane again." That was Colin.

"Do you have another idea?" argued the man called Grant.

"Look, I'm just saying we'll have to find people who know what they're doing."

"What about the people that were in the scouting party?" asked Jane.

"Why don't all of us just rip the plane apart?" asked Cut-Glass gruffly.

"Wif what?" shot back Colin.

"Hey, hey, hostility won't help anybody," Grant said.

"*What* is up with you?" asked Cut-Glass, responding to Grant.

"What are you talking about?"

"Just because you're a pretty-boy with a tie and a government job, you think you're better than us?"

"Guys," said Jane, "This isn't what we need to be focused on. We're not alone, and whoever is out there might be hostile. We need to focus on getting out of here."

"The Voice of Wisdom," muttered Cut-Glass.

"Look, Darby, I don't know what your problem is," said Grant to Cut-Glass, "but if you can't handle working with people I suggest you find your own way off the island."

"Do you mean besides letting a blind kid handle our radio?" Apparently, Cut-Glass's name was Darby. "What if he messes it up?"

"I won't," I spoke up. It was about time someone knew I was standing there.

"If you work for the government, Grant," began Jane, obviously unconcerned about my being in their pow-wow, "why can't you work a transmitter?"

"I'm not a field-agent. I have an office job for the CIA. Basically I sign papers all day," he said quietly. He must have been embarrassed.

"Technically," I cut in, "anybody could make the transmitter work. It isn't too difficult. It's just that no one wants to screw it up." Obviously my words had a small effect on them. They were quiet for a while.

"He's right," said Colin. "Well, meeting's over."

They shuffled away, and Jane walked up to me. "If you'd like to be by the rest of us," she offered, "I could set you up there."

"Thanks." It was kind of cold in my place by the trees, and lonely to boot.

As we neared the camp, I felt the warmth of the fire and heard people talking indistinctly. Jane sat me down and told me I was by trees again. She also got me a blanket. "Thank you," I said, and I really meant it.

"Sure, Rick. Good-night."

"Good-night." I leaned back against a tree-trunk. I dreaded the morning, when whether we got rescued or not kind of depended on me. But right now I was warm and tired, which made for a good night's sleep.

Chapter 4

Day Five began very early. Paul shook me awake. "Grant told me to get you up," he said. "People are in a hurry to get the transmitter working."

"Fine," I said grumpily. "Tell them I won't work on it until I've had some proper sleep."

"Uhhh…"

I shook my head. "Kidding, Paul, kidding. Help me up." I extended my arm and he dragged me to a standing position. "I should have stayed in my cubbyhole where no one could find me," I sighed.

"Sorry about that, man. These guys are pumped. They're trying to find stuff to dig through the plane with. When the front part broke off and slid down the beach it hit some big rocks and like, imploded."

"It's okay." I yawned and rubbed my eyes. "Do I look like a wreck? I feel like one."

"Actually, dude…you look pretty bad. Your clothes are ripped up and your shirt's full of blood. Your face is kinda grimy. Your forehead is messed up."

"I sound positively gruesome."

"You are, kinda."

"If I could find my luggage, I could get some new clothes. Thank goodness I don't have to shave yet. I'd cut myself to pieces now."

"I brought you breakfast." He handed me something thin and squishy.

"What is it?" I asked with trepidation.

"An energy bar. They're about the only food we got left."

It tasted like sugared candle-wax, but it was enough to settle my stomach. "You know, Paul," I said when I was done, "what I could really use is a hot shower. Do people bathe in the ocean or what?"

"I just jumped in and swam around in some shorts."

"Great idea. How close are they to getting into the plane?"

"Um, they're just arguing right now."

"Good. Lead on to the ocean, Paul."

I had said I wanted a hot shower, and what I got was a cold bath. Paul led me away from the other passengers to a calmer part of the ocean.

"I feel like one of those older people who do those thera-peutic swims," I said as I peeled off my shoes and socks.

"Why?" asked Paul.

"Because you're toting me around like an invalid and you have to watch me."

"I'm not even very good at it."

"Well, thanks for doing it. Why are you doing it?"

"I kind of have nothing else to do," he said bluntly. "Besides, you're getting us out of here."

"If you ever want a reference for being a nurse or a chauffer, you call me."

I was hesitant to take off my shirt, knowing how pale I was. I wasn't what you'd call buff, either. My stomach had a little baby fat which shouldn't count as baby fat anymore. "How far away from the others are we?"

"Pretty far. Yo, I'm gonna nap. You mind?"

"Go ahead."

"You sure?"

"Yeah." In reality, I wished he'd lead me in. But I shouldn't bother him.

I took off my shirt and carefully stepped into the surf in my pants. After a half hour I was handling being waist-deep in the water. It was scary, being in water and not seeing it. I was never a good swimmer. If I was breaking myself into the world of the blind, this was a great start. I couldn't be afraid of much after this.

After a while I dunked my head under and came back up. I didn't account for the saltwater seeping into the cut on my forehead. It stung like crazy. I rubbed my body with water and dunked again.

I lost my footing and slipped. My heart skipped a few beats as the current pummeled me. I bounced back up again, breathing hard, and immediately felt my way back to the beach with my feet. I lay on the sand, panting and shivering, not from cold. I shouldn't have done it alone. I could have drowned and no one would have been the wiser.

"What are you supposed to be?" asked a very Barbie voice.

My heart sank in utter despair. First I almost drown, now I'm dying of humiliation. "A dead jellyfish," I said without emotion. I'd been discovered.

"Are you that blind kid?" Barbie asked. I could picture the disdain on her zit-free face.

"Yes, I am." Why did people have to describe me like that?

"Oh. I'm sorry."

"Sure you are. Is there a guy napping nearby?" I didn't care if I had to ask her something so simple. I was too shaken and embarrassed to care.

"Not really."

"That's helpful. What are you doing over here?"

"Tanning."

I smelled the overwhelming coconutty scent of tanning lotion. "Why?"

"That's a dumb question."

I didn't explain myself. "What time is it?"

"I don't know. Shouldn't you be with the guys looking for the transmitter?"

"Shouldn't you be on the set of Baywatch?" I said. This girl's kind of attitude was what I'd have to face when I got back to the real world. People who looked down on me because they thought I was a weakling. "You're right. I should be out there saving your skinny rear. If I could just find my nurse…"

"Do you need help?"

I cringed at the way she said it. "Hey, PAUL!" I shouted obnoxiously.

I heard someone running. "Dude!" Paul panted, "You totally freaked me out! I thought you'd drowned."

"Today's my lucky day. Where's my shirt?"

"Oh, since you seemed okay in the water, I went over to my luggage and got you one of my shirts. Yours was history. When I came back, I couldn't find you." He gave me a t-shirt and I put it on gratefully. "I'm Paul." I heard him introduce himself to Barbie.

"I'm Dana," she said snootily, and must have walked away.

"Ouch!" said Paul.

"The Queen has left the premises," I said with a sigh. "Paul, please take me back to the others. I have to go work a transmitter."

When we made it back, Paul told me the wrecking crew was already working on the plane. "I'm also helping with getting into the plane," he said, "so I'll be close by if you need me."

"Good. See you later." Woops. Bad line.

"Hey, Rick." It was Jane. "They're digging through the remains now."

"If they just started doing that, why did Grant have Paul wake me up ages ago?"

"Did he? He thinks he has some sort of strategy going."

"Did the hunting party head out yet?"

"Yeah. They were led by Professor Taylor."

"The chemistry guy?"

"He says he lived in the wild for a while and he can hunt."

"Who went with him?"

"Colin, a guy named Kurt, and a couple rough-looking men. I'll be surprised if they don't catch something."

"Everyone else wanted to be here for the Big Moment, huh?"

"Uh-huh."

"Who am I giving orders to?"

"Grant didn't say."

"Who is this Grant guy, anyway, and why is he suddenly the Emperor of Survivors?"

"In a crisis like this, someone who acts like they're in charge is a relief. It feels like things are in control when you have only a few people heading things up."

"I get the impression Colin and Grant are tied for leader. Doctors are always respected."

"Well, an intern will do in a pinch." Her voice, as usual, was soft and subdued. It felt like there was something else she wanted to say.

"Hey, Jane-" I began.

"Rick!" Grant advanced upon us and my chance to talk to Jane was gone. "They're breaking through to the cockpit now. You ready?"

"Sure."

"I thought you could tell me how to use the transmitter."

41

"Uh, I was thinking of telling Jane, actually."

He paused. "Jane has no previous experience with this kind of thing."

Jane started to say something, but stopped.

"And you do?" I asked him.

"No."

"So...I pick Jane."

"Why?" he asked.

"Because I can talk to her easier."

There was another pause. "Okay," surrendered Grant. "It's Jane."

Jane led me through the wreck. It was awful. I fell on her multiple times and cut myself on sharp metal twice. "My balance is nil," I said in an apologetic way.

"It's okay. Nothing in here is level any more."

The smell of burned metal and plastic wasn't as bad as the smell of rot. Though the rot was fainter, it churned my stomach.

We paused. "Are there...bodies...in here...?" I asked.

"There were. Remember when you were stuck in that pile of them?" she asked quietly.

"Yeah."

"Those were the ones we could get out of the plane and some that died when they were thrown onto the beach. We burned them. They took the bodies out of here a little while ago, and they'll probably burn them, too."

"What...did you do with Noah's body?"

"We buried him and the co-pilot in the woods. We carved their names in wood as grave-markers."

"Thank you." I wouldn't ask to visit the grave. I didn't believe in all that sentimental stuff. Noah died and was gone. He was better off in Heaven, anyway.

"Hey, Jane," I heard someone call. "We just broke through the door. There's a body in here. We'll get it out."

"How?"

"Maybe we can break through the nose. The windshield thing is broken, but the roof must've collapsed when we hit the ground. It's like one crumpled ball in there."

"Just bring it back this way," Jane ordered. There was some of that strength again.

There was a time of grunting and pulling and hammering, and finally we stepped aside to let them carry the body through. I heard the workers file past. "Good luck, man," I heard Paul say to me.

"The body - what'd she look like?" I asked Jane before we moved on.

"How did you know it was a woman?"

I only shrugged.

"Blonde...I can't say, really. She was all...she was very..."

I pushed a grotesque picture of a mangled Gwen out of my mind. "Did she have a uniform on?"

"Yes." I could tell by her voice she knew that I knew who it was. "Was she a close friend?"

"She was going to be my sister-in-law," I said sadly.

We stumbled to the cockpit in silence. Jane propped me against the control panel. The plane was more twisted out of shape than I thought. I knew because the buttons and switches that should have been at waist-height dug into my shoulder. I knew for sure the plane radio was definitely busted, then. When I breathed I smelled death. I refused to imagine what my surroundings looked like.

"Where, um, where's the-" Jane gagged.

"What?" I covered my nose with my arm.

"There's blood, and, uh, it...where's the transmitter?"

"It should be behind the jump-seat."

There were lots of moving sounds. "Ugh," Jane said hoarsely.

"What now?"

"I'm trying to get the seat out of the way and it's covered in…augh, this is sick."

My stomach rolled at the thought of it. "I'm sorry."

"Hello in there!" shouted an annoyingly leisurely voice. It was Grant. "Everything okay? I came to give you some help. What the-?" He choked. "What's that smell?"

"Expired life," I said painfully.

"Help me," Jane groaned. There was lots of digging around and a few cuss words they let slip. I didn't blame them.

"It's not here." Jane heaved a sigh.

"It has to be here," Grant mumbled. They shuffled around. "Hey!" he yelled. "What's this?"

"We didn't do that. I don't think the crew did, either," Jane said.

"What's up?" I asked.

"There's a flap cut into the metal on the side of the plane by the pilot's seat," Jane said.

"Are you sure it's man-made?"

"Yes," Grant murmured. "It's cut a little too cleanly and rounded not to be."

There was a period of confused silence. *Why would someone cut a hole in the cockpit?* I thought. "Is it big enough for a man to fit through?"

"Yeah."

Did someone take the transmitter? I thought, alarmed. "Is anything else missing?"

"I couldn't tell," Grant said. "Let's look again. It has to be here."

"Wish I could help you." They were too busy to hear me. I waited for them, wishing I were anywhere but here in the Pit of Death. I thought I might be sick again. I was sweating and knew Jane and Grant must be also. After a long time, they stopped working. "It's not here," Jane announced. "C'mon, Grant, let's get out of here."

"Wait, wait," he pleaded. "We have to keep looking."

"It isn't here, Grant," Jane repeated, taking on her firm tone. "If we stay here any longer, we'll get sick."

"I am sick," I piped up.

"We'll get some workers in here, then," Grant suggested.

"Grant, it isn't here." She was firm but not angry. "Please, c'mon, let's just go."

"What am I supposed to tell them?" Grant said in anguish. "Those people out there think we're bringing help to them."

"It isn't your fault someone took it," I said.

"Who said someone took it?" Grant asked.

"Why do you think someone cut that flap?" pointed out Jane. "Somebody doesn't want us to get off this island. They took the transmitter."

"But – that make no sense," Grant sighed. "Who wouldn't want out of here?"

"Let's leave here through the flap," Jane said, ignoring the question. "We can catch our breath before we have to face the others."

They had an awkward time shoving me through the hole. We landed on sand. I was never so glad to be outside. I gulped in great drinks of fresh air and listened to the waves, not so far away.

"So..." Grant spoke after a time. "Should we tell them yet?" Despair didn't begin to describe the sound in our voices.

"Wait another minute," Jane said tiredly. "And when we do tell them, I don't think we should mention the flap."

"Good idea," Grant agreed. "So what's your occupation, Jane?" He suddenly seemed so friendly. I hadn't expected it from him.

Jane hesitated. "It's pretty boring. I work for an insurance company."

"You don't look it."

"Thanks, I think." She laughed. So did he. I wondered what she looked like and regretted not having asked before.

"What do you do, Rick?" asked Grant. "I mean…do you have a job?"

"Too young."

"Just school, then?"

I nodded.

"What's your dad do?"

"Nothing."

"No job?"

"He's dead. So is my mom."

"Oh." I heard him shift around uncomfortably. "Jane told us about your brother, the pilot, when we buried him." He sounded sorry.

"You were in the scouting party?"

"Yeah. I may be a pretty boy with a government job, but I did my fair share of CIA training." His laugh was nice enough.

"And you don't know about transmitters?" I asked quizzically.

"Yeah, well…I didn't actually finish the training…in fact I didn't get very far at all…" He waited to go on. "I guess you don't know, but I have a paralyzed hand."

I didn't know, couldn't have known. I guess he said that for my benefit, and I supposed I should respond. "How'd it happen?"

"Well…it was an accident. My buddy and I were in a crash."

"Car crash?" Jane asked quietly.

"Yeah. My friend died." By his voice, I could tell he missed his friend.

I felt a strange bond with him now. "My parents died in a car crash," I said.

Grant went on. "I couldn't be a field agent with my disability, so they made me a paper-pusher instead. Not as fun, but I still serve my country."

"What were you doing on the flight?" Jane asked him.

"Working out some kinks over in London. Taking a bullet for something we did to offend the Brits. Those people are rough. What were you doing in England, Jane?"

"Visiting relatives."

Ouch. I smiled as Grant sort of stuttered through an explanation about how he guessed British folks aren't all that rough.

We lay in the sand; at least I assumed they were laying like I was, for a little longer.

"We probably won't get out of here very soon," Grant said slowly. "I'd like to thank you guys for trying to find the transmitter."

"Jane tried," I pointed out.

"But you wanted to help us work it."

I felt honored.

"Guess we have to tell them now..." he said slowly. He evidently walked away.

"We'll be there in a minute," Jane called to him. I was glad, because I wanted to talk to her. "So Grant isn't as bad as he seems," Jane said quietly, after, I assumed, Grant had left.

"He just has control issues." I paused. "Jane..." I started, and didn't know what to say next. Finally, "Jane, I feel like there's something you need to tell someone." It sounded so stupid. I grimaced.

"I do," she said, surprising me. "How'd you know?"

"Your voice, the way you act..."

She laughed quietly. "Because I yelled at you?"

"Partly."

"I'm sorry. It's just...I lost someone too, once, and I was getting mad at myself, not you." She got rid of the quiet voice and took on a regular tone. It sounded better. "There's a reason, Rick, that I can't tell you why I'm like that. I guess I'll give up the little schoolgirl act. It's not me."

"Why were you doing it in the first place?"

"I'll tell you why later, maybe."

"Okay." I was disappointed, and tried not to show it.

She let out a long breath. "You're a good kid, Rick. I'm sorry I was so weird to you."

I nodded glumly and wished people would stop calling me a 'kid.' "We should go help Grant bear up under probable persecution and mutiny," I said wryly, changing the subject.

As we walked back, I considered what reason Jane could have to put on act.

Chapter 5

When we reached the group, the passengers were just beginning to throw colorful words around, mostly in Grant's direction.

"Listen!" he said firmly, "there's no reason to attack me. If you want to go look for it yourselves, you're welcome. But it isn't there."

"How are supposed to get out of here?!" someone yelled.

"I don't know," Grant said simply. "But I'm sure we'll find some way of doing it. Right now, it might be a good idea to search the surrounding area in case the transmitter was thrown from the plane."

The group broke up with frustrated murmurings.

"Well, that went better than I thought," Grant mused seriously.

"Do you really think the transmitter is lost somewhere?" Jane asked.

"No," he said with a sigh. "I think you guys are probably right and someone took it. But I still ask, why? Who would want to stay here so bad, and at the same time strand everyone else with them?"

"A psycho person," I said. "So on top of everything else, we have a nut case running around loose." In the pause that followed, I wondered whether it bothered them that I was in on all of this. I was in the know now, in the circle of people who were kind of in charge. If they did mind, they'd have to tell me, because I couldn't see if they were giving me any dirty looks.

"Rick is right," Jane said. "We should be careful."

"Well...it's not like they're going to shoot somebody or something dangerous. I don't think we had any guns or other weapons on board...did we?"

"I don't know," I shrugged.

"Would there be some kind of record?" he asked.

"If you're asking me," I said, "I have no idea. I'm new to all this airline stuff."

"Speaking of records," continued Grant, "should we find the flight manifest?"

"What for?" asked Jane.

"To check who's here and who isn't."

"Again, what for?"

"To know who died or not, so we can tell their families."

"Don't you think when they don't come back, their families will know?"

"Do you have a problem with this?"

"No."

There was a doubtful pause. "If we find the manifest and know who's here, we can do a roll call now and then to make sure no one's missing. Rick, do you know where it is?"

I realized then that I had been labeled (along with some other things) 'Airplane Boy,' and was expected to know everything about airplanes and their procedures. I wasn't about to point out I knew as little as anybody else. My title gave me good standing in the Inner Circle. All I said was, "Maybe it's in the front of the plane, where the staff would be."

"Good idea."

"Won't it be burned?" countered Jane.

Grant sniffed, and I pictured him grimacing. "Yeah, probably."

"What time is it?" Jane asked.

"Uh, about…a quarter to twelve." He must have checked his watch. "Why?"

"Shouldn't we start handing out food now?"

"Yeah, we'll look for the manifest later. Bye, Rick."

"Here." Jane took my arm and led me back to my spot. "We give out rations about now. I'll get yours."

"Thanks. Whose idea was that? The rationing thing?"

"It was Colin's idea, but Grant decides how much we get."

"They don't get along well, do they?" She didn't answer, and I guessed she left. I sat and waited for my food, which turned out to be beef jerky and fruit leather. My teeth and jaw protested strongly, but my stomach was happy when I was done. I started dreaming about the pies Aunt Sandy used to make. And then I wondered why it was that all aunts were destined to make a continuous line of good pies. I was deep in this thought when Paul came to sit by me.

"Hey, dude."

"Hi there."

"So…big bummer, huh? No transmitter." He sounded glum.

"Yeah. Hey, Paul, does your aunt make pies?"

"What?"

"Um, never mind, I tend to mull over quirks of fate. Are you busy right now?"

"No."

"Will you do something for me?"

"Sure. What's up?"

"I'd like to learn to walk without keeling over on everybody. Can you walk me along the beach 'til I get the hang of it?"

"Yeah, sure thing."

51

Finding my balance was the hardest part, especially on sand. Paul wanted to smooth a path out for me, but I said if I learned to walk on lumpy sand I could walk on anything.

We were away from everyone, on a clear part that Paul had described as going 'on and on.' I held on to his arm for a few laps up and down the beach, and then when I got used to the feel, I held on to his hand. By that time I was tired and determined to walk on my own. I could tell how far we had walked by listening to the surf going in and out. I knew that I knew that I wouldn't run into anything, but my body was saying I would.

As I let go of Paul's hand, with him encouraging me and walking alongside in case, I took my first wobbly steps of freedom. My movements were jerky and painfully slow. But I made it to our lap marker, a stick in the sand.

"You did it, man!" said Paul happily. "You did it!"

"Let's do it again." We did. I felt sorry for Paul, who had to be bored, but I was too determined to quit. Paul ended up staying at one end and cheering so I could hear where I was going, and I walked to the stick and back so many times that I finally walked normally (as normally as you can walk on lumpy sand).

I eventually surrendered and decided I'd done enough for one day. Paul grabbed me and hugged me. "You did it! You did it, little man! You so rock!"

"We did it," I said. For the first time since Noah died I felt I had a brother again.

"Dude, you so totally deserve an award for, like, most perseverant person or something."

"You deserve an award for the best friend a blind guy could have," I said as we trudged back. I was holding on to his arm, but didn't mind. He was just steering me, and I was walking on my own. I never thought I'd be so happy just to walk.

When we got back, people were having another get together.

"They should be back by now," someone moaned.

"Are we supposed to eat chocolate bars for dinner or what?"

"We sure waited long enough to go hunting. I said from day one-"

"Maybe they were eaten by whatever's out there."

People were edgy, I could hear that. I couldn't tell which they wanted most: to leave this place, eat, or get the hunting group back. To the majority of the passengers, number three was probably small beans. I myself worried the hunters were lost. Or worse.

I thought Grant would deliver another silver-lining speech, but he must have given up on that. In fact, he made things worse. "We don't have enough rations left to give everyone tonight," he announced. "We'll have to divide what's left amongst ourselves."

"What do you mean, there's not enough left?" I recognized Darby, the cut-glass guy. "Who was in charge of keeping track of them?"

"Frankly, we all were," said Grant roughly. "But I was the one counting."

"So what, you can't count?" sneered Darby.

"There just wasn't enough!"

"And it's your fault!" Darby argued. "If you were counting them, why didn't you tell us before?"

"Because I didn't find it necessary to start a panic! I wasn't the only one who waited until day five to look for food. And, I thought the hunters would be back by now."

"You didn't consult any of us, did you?" a woman shouted. "It was our food, too!"

"Yeah," said Darby, "who died and made you king?"

Jane spoke up. "Grant isn't in charge here. He's not your leader. But you all act like he is when you want one and point fingers at him when you don't want one. Yes, he was in charge of the food, and he screwed up, but the rest of you could have checked out the supplies any time you wanted."

Silence followed, and I guess they were all thinking Jane was right. I was thinking there was something fishy going on. There was no way Grant would have waited until the last minute to do something about the food. He was too precise. He would have had a back up plan or something.

"Hey, Paul," I said, "Will you take me to Jane? I have to talk to her."

Paul guided me over and said he'd see me later.

"What's up?" asked Jane curiously.

"Is Grant around?"

"Right here," he said.

"Are we alone?"

"Yeah, Jane's speech dispersed the crowd."

"So…what was all that about?"

"What do you mean?" asked Grant evasively.

"Grant, there is no way the food just happened to run out," I said.

He sighed. "Someone is stealing again."

I nodded. "That's what I thought."

"Is this as confusing to you guys as it is to me?" asked Jane. "Assuming the person who stole the food is the same person who stole the transmitter, his two crimes don't add up."

"What?"

"If he stole the transmitter to stay on the island, why would he take the food, too? The food would keep us here longer."

"You're right."

Suddenly, I had an idea. "Hey, guys?" I said quietly, the thought still forming.

"I pity the hunting party," Jane sighed. "If they didn't find food, they're in serious trouble."

"Guys?" I said again.

"They better have found food," Grant said. "We can't survive on this island without it. People are already hungry. I can't imagine what we'll do if-"

"Guys!"

"What?"

"We think the thief is someone in this camp."

"Yeah…"

"What if it isn't? What if whatever we heard last night were inhabitants of this place and what if those natives decided to come into our camp and take some stuff?"

"When would they have done that?" asked Grant.

"Any time."

"But we would have seen them. We're spread out everywhere, and we have people up at night feeding the fires. Plus, why would they steal a transmitter?" Grant asked.

I felt the heat of embarrassment creeping up my neck. "Well…it was just an idea," I mumbled. *I should have thought it out more and kept my mouth shut. They probably think I'm too eager to prove I'm as smart as they are.*

"We should keep Rick's idea in mind," Jane said, easing a bit of the embarrassment. "Right now, we have no more clues."

"Right."

"Have you found the flight manifest yet?" I asked, changing the subject abruptly.

"Jane looked, but couldn't find anything."

"Rick, I'll get your food," Jane said. She took my arm and led me to my spot as if she led a blind boy around every day.

Paul came and sat by me a little later. "Those dried oranges really hit the spot, huh?"

I made a face.

"Somethin' bothering you, dude?"

"Many, many things are bothering me right now," I said shortly. "Thank you for asking, but there's nothing you can do." I cocked my head. "Well, actually, there is. What does Jane look like? I know you're sick of having to describe things to me, but-"

"Dude," he cut in.

"Yeah...you have nothing else to do."

"It's totally cool, dude. If something bothers me, I'll let you know."

"Okay."

"Alriiiight." He let out a long breath. "How do you picture her?"

"Brown hair, brown eyes, non-descript, you know? On the skinny side."

"Okay, she's, like, one of those natural looking girls. You know, that look like they go running and hiking and climbing and stuff?"

"Hmm."

"She's not too muscular, but toned, I would say. Honey-cinnamon blonde hair, down to her shoulders. Brown eyes. Her skin is medium tone. A little taller than you, but not much."

My surprise must have shown on my face.

"Not how you pictured her?" Paul said with a laugh.

"Totally not. I had her pinned as a...seriously, a Plain Jane. I didn't think she was *beautiful*."

"She's not beau-" He paused thoughtfully. "Well, I guess you're right. If she didn't walk around looking so harsh all the time, she might be really pretty."

"You know what's weird? She said I looked like her little brother."

"I'm totally not seeing the resemblance between you and her. When did she say that?"

"She...she thought I was...she thought that I thought she was..."

"You had a crush on her or what?"

"She was probably using it as a defense mechanism," I said slowly, reasoning it out. "I asked her how old she was, and she took it the wrong way and asked if I was hitting on her, and I denied it profusely and she said, 'Good'-"

"'You look *just* like my little brother,'" he said in a mocking girly voice. "Dude, that is terrible. I've had that happen."

"Why do girls do that?"

"They're sending you a message. Obviously no girl even likes her little brother, so there's no point in liking her."

"They shouldn't do that to us. It's just wrong. She was making sure I knew my place. She most likely hasn't got a little brother."

"I doubt it."

"She thinks I'm a little freak, I just know it." I hid my face in my hands, as if I could hide from the world.

"I thought she was nice to you."

"Augh!" I groaned. "I am a little freak, that's the problem."

"But a very cute little freak." He was trying to make me feel better.

I raised my head and took a deep breath. "I agonize over things too much."

"Yeah, you do."

I would have given him a dirty look, but that wouldn't work now. "Oh, forget it. I can't change the past. Describe Grant and Colin for me. Please."

"You have to play the game. How do you picture Mr. CIA?"

"Average height, blonde hair, blue eyes, the real dashing sort."

"He does look dashing. Blonde? You really think he's blonde? He isn't. He's, like, got reddish-brownish hair that's always combed the right way even though we're on an island, like. I don't know about his eye color."

"Would you say Grant was a 'pretty boy'?"

"Uh, I always thought that was a demeaning term to use for a grown man. Okay, now describe Colin."

"Hmm. I don't really know. Tall. His voice sounds high up."

"Right. Tall, dark wavy hair, green eyes, rugged features. Like the opposite of Grant."

I nodded. "You should be an artist."

"I am. Like, on the side, in my spare time."

"Is there anything you can't do?" I didn't wait for him to answer. "You know what I want to know? If Grant and Colin are their last names or their first names."

"Yeah...you think about the strangest things."

"Gee, thanks." I didn't disagree with him. He was right.

Chapter 6

Day Six dawned, a windy and sour day. I could feel people's frowns as they walked by me. Their voices were low and harsh.

The lady named Rita came by to see me. She brought me a couple figs. "It's me, Rita," she announced when she came. "Remember me?"

"Sure I do."

"This is the only kind of food we have left," she huffed as she sat beside me. By her voice, I judged her to be in her late fifties. She seemed the motherly type.

"Thank you." I ate the figs slowly, to make them last. "How are you?"

"I'm fine, but I think the rest of 'em are pretty grumpy. No huntin' party yet, though I pray they get back safe."

"Are you from Texas, Ma'am?" I asked.

"Sure! How'd you know?"

"Your accent."

"Gives me away every time." She laughed a full, hearty laugh. "People in England were de-lighted by my accent. They thought it was the cutest thang."

"Why were you in London?"

"My rich grandson sent me out there for some rest and relaxation. He thinks I'm gettin' old and need all that junk, thank goodness. Most exhilarating time of my life." She made a contented noise. "Why were you there?"

"I was with my brother. He was the airplane captain." It still hurt to talk about Noah.

"Oh! He was the poor young man that the scoutin' party found, wasn't he? Yes, I heard about that. I'm sorry."

"It's alright." Did everybody know my business? What was this, Big Brother?

"Where'd you go in London?" Rita asked.

"I got to see Big Ben and ride a double-decker bus. That was about all. We don't – we didn't - usually have enough time to sight-see whenever we made a stop anywhere. Where did you go?"

Rita spent a very long time telling me about the health spa she went to just outside of London, in a "quaint little English town with a funny little name."

Then she told me about her life in Texas, but had the manners and feelings to leave my own life story alone. She could talk a person's ear off, but she was really nice.

Later, lunch consisted of a large helping of nothing, as did dinner. There was a box of figs left, it was said, but we were apparently saving that for an emergency.

Night came, and I worried about the hunting party. I asked God to let them get back safely, and if possible, to bring a lot of food. I was still confused at God, but he had at least granted me life, even if it was a terrible life at the moment.

Paul came by to tell me they'd set up a rope, like a railing, to lead to the john, in case someone had to go at night, so I could find it by myself if I needed to. Later on, I needed to. It's a good feeling when you can use the facilities on your own.

Walking back, with the rope guiding me, I heard an odd noise. A sniffling sound, coming from the forest. The curiosity bug bit me and I ducked under the rope. Still holding on, I edged towards the sound. I felt a tree in front of me. The sound came from behind the tree. I stepped on a branch and it cracked. The sniffling sound stopped. "Who's there?" a whimpering voice asked.

"Sorry," I said hoarsely. I realized the person was crying. "I didn't see you. I'm going away now." I ducked under the rope and walked away, but not before I smelled coconut-scented tanning lotion.

Day Seven arrived, and with it, a lot of hunger and anger. I heard three fights break out. People were really edgy. Fortunately, someone had the brains to go explore in a different direction and discovered fruit trees. Breakfast was an opportunity for peace.

Paul came by to tell me he'd helped find an opening to the cargo area of the plane, which had become embedded in the sand. Some people's tempers had been restored somewhat by the return of their belongings. Unfortunately, the cargo area had ripped open during our descent to ground, so not all the luggage was in the plane. They were going to take a group of people to look for it, as well as the missing transmitter. I wondered over the last part. What was Grant's angle on doing that? Restoring people's hope?

"Grant wants you to come, dude, in case they actually find the transthingie."

My eyebrows shot up. "Airplane Boy to the rescue," I murmured.

"What'd you say?"

"Nothing."

"We're gonna restock on drinking water, too. Hey...I got this for you." He laid something heavy in my hands.

"What is it?"

"A stick," he said, with a proud voice.

"Okay..."

"Like those sticks people who can't see use to walk. You know, so you won't run into anything. I used my pocket knife to smooth it up a bit."

Suddenly, a strange emotion overtook me. "You...you made me a stick. Thanks." My eyes tingled. I cleared my throat and stood up. The stick was the right height. It was strong and straight, and I held it above the ground a little, trying to recall how I'd seen blind people hold them in movies. If I had this, I wouldn't have to drag along on someone's arm all the time.

"How is it?" Paul asked.

I smiled, the first time in a long time that I'd done so. It spread across my face. It felt wonderful. I had a stick in my hands, but it felt like I was holding Excalibur.

"Dude! You're smiling!"

"Paul, I hope you don't mind my saying this, but you're the best friend I've got."

I heard him laugh. I pictured his smile. "Hey, dude, it's worth it." He ruffled my hair.

"I owe you one."

"Aw, forget it."

I wouldn't ever forget.

The scouting group gathered right after a small lunch of fruit.

Grant, as was expected, was heading it up. I laughed inwardly at human traditions that made us want one man to be in charge of everything. At least Grant was doing well.

"Okay!" he shouted. "Roll call! I don't want to leave anybody behind."

"Jane."

"Paul."

"Darby."

"Dana."

Dana? I thought. A.k.a. *Queen of the Beach? A.k.a. the Girl That Cries in the Woods?* She didn't strike me as the hiking type. "Rick," I said.

"Karen." I didn't know Karen.

"Zack." I didn't know him, either.

"Alright," Grant continued, "since it's getting darker, we're going to be tied to each other just in case."

Oh, that's reassuring. If a wild animal attacks one of us, we can all go down together. Grant's idea was actually a good one, I knew. No one could stray and get lost. It was especially nice for me.

But why did he say it was getting dark, and so early? Having an idea, I sniffed in a bunch of air. I smelled rain. *Great. Grant had to pick me to be Airplane Boy. Why do I have to go on this silly walk? I'd rather hide under a tarp.* This whole hike sounded wet and dangerous. I think I minded the wet part more than the danger.

"Can I ask why you're going?" I heard Grant say to someone.

Dana answered in an annoyed voice. "My bag has been missing since day one, and I cannot stand another minute without my stuff. You have no idea how difficult it is to be so unhygienic. So I'm going whether you like it or not."

"Where'd you get the suntan lotion?" asked Karen.

"It was in my carry-on bag. I wear it all the time." She changed the subject. "So I'm going," she said again.

"Okay." Obviously, he didn't approve.

We were tied in a certain order. Grant in the lead (of course), then Dana, Paul, Zack, Karen, me, and Jane. I took my stick in case I would need it, using it as a walking stick.

Grant announced we were going northwest (he was either good at directions or he had a compass). We crossed open fields. I felt a sharp wind on my face and heard grass waving. The fields were hilly and hard to walk over when tied to six other people. When Grant stopped to get his bearings, Jane described what they were looking at. "There's a mountain range in front of us, but it looks like there might be something else taller beyond that. West there's some sparse trees, with a forest to the right of them, east is some more fields, and south is our camp."

I was confused. Why had it been so easy for her to describe everything? Had her silliness in attempting and failing to describe things before been part of her act? Why, oh why did she have to be so frustratingly mysterious?

"Rick? You alright?"

"Sure. I was just thinking."

We went west, towards the cave that the scouting party had found. We went through the trees, which were few and far between, and found a small pool created by the spring. Beyond it was a giant cave. (Jane told me all this).

We went around the pool and stopped at the cave, where we untied the rope connecting us. "Okay," said Grant, "the scouting party searched around the cave the last time we were here, but we didn't search the cliffs behind it. I think we should try that way, since the plane came in from the west, behind the cliffs. I think two people should stay behind and get drinking water. Dana, Rick, you guys do that."

"Whoooaaa, hold it," Dana said angrily. "I am not about to sit around baby sitting a blind kid while you guys go have fun."

I clenched my jaw and wished I could bash her pretty nose in for the way she talked about me.

"We won't have fun," Grant answered her sharply. "We're crossing a ravine at the back of the cave and then climbing up a cliff. By the time we get up there we'll be sweaty and tired and full of bruises."

That statement settled it for Miss Supermodel. "Fine, I'll stay here."

"I should warn you," I said, "my naptime is coming up soon and I'll be cranky without my teddy bear." I heard a few snorts of laughter.

"Ha-ha," Dana said with a definite sneer.

The rest of the group gave us two backpacks full of water-bottles and Dana and I sat near the pool. "You fill them, I'll put them back in the bags," she ordered.

"Sure, you tell me when they're full. Because, you know, I can't see them." I was really, really steamed at her, and hoped she knew it.

I dipped the bottles in the water and she said "When" when they were full. I capped them and handed them back. I wondered whether Grant had been trying to get rid of her when he told her to do this. I knew he was thinking of a way to leave me behind, too, without hurting my feelings. There was no way I could climb up a cliff. I wondered a little bit how Grant himself could do it with only one good hand, and figured he must just use that annoying drive in him to do what he set his mind to.

After the forty bottles were filled, Dana had trouble getting them arranged in the backpacks again. I hear her grunting and shoving and shaking the bags.

"Want help?" I asked.

"And what could you do?"

"I could arrange them as well as you can. You don't have to see them." She dumped the bag in my lap and I took all the bottles out and put them back strategically. It was hard to do when I could only feel them, but after traveling across the world, I knew how to pack things in a bag pretty well. With an air of triumph, I zipped up the backpack and successfully filled the other bag as well. "You're welcome."

"Hooray for you."

I shook my head and leaned back to lie in the grass.

"So…we have to wait for them, or what? How long are they going to take?" She was clearly going to play the bored-to-death card.

"We could explore the cave," I suggested.

"No way."

"Scared of bats?"

"No. I don't want to have to drag you around behind me."

"Thanks for wanting to be helpful, but I could walk on my own."

"Right. Can you run on your own, too? Why don't we go play tag in the fields?"

"I think blind tag would be more appropriate." I could play her sarcasm game, and beat her, too.

"You are such a freak."

Well, that was three people, including myself, who thought so. "It's better than being a jerk," I countered. "Have you ever considered that even freaks have feelings?"

"Are you going to cry again?"

I frowned. "What do you mean, 'again'?"

"I heard you crying, those first few days after we crashed."

"I wasn't crying, I was…" She had me pinned for a minute. "I wasn't exactly having the time of my life."

"Neither was I."

"No? Did you get buried under a pile of dead bodies, lose your memory, find out your brother and friends were dead, and on top of that go blind?"

"I suppose you were cursed by an evil grandmother or something…you're so exaggerating."

"Hardly. My mom and dad and brother have all died. Besides…you cried, too."

By her silence, I knew I was right. "I thought you didn't see me."

"I smelled you. Your, uh, tanning lotion."

"Oh. Well, I guess that makes us even."

"I guess." I dug the heel of my shoe into the ground to vent some frustration.

"You look upset."

"I'm not." I refused to get emotional.

She sighed. "Where'd you get that big gash on your head?"

"What're you going to do now, tell me I'm ugly on top of being a freak?"

She made a confused sound. "Can't I ask a simple question?"

I shook my head again. "Look, I don't know why you decided to hate me in particular, but your attitude doesn't make for leisurely conversation."

"What made you think I hate you?" she asked, like it was so obvious that she didn't.

"Gee, how about how, since you met me, every other word out of your mouth is an insult? Do you not realize we've been at each other for the past hour or so?"

"I wasn't fighting with you. You care too much."

"Why are you even arguing with me? You're the adult. Act like one."

"What exactly makes me the adult? We're, like, the same age."

"And how old are you?"

"Nineteen."

I was in shock. "You're only nineteen?"

"Well, how old are you?"

I sat up. "Fourteen."

"What?" She sounded startled. "But – you don't look fourteen. I thought you were older."

"Everybody does. Why did you call me a kid?"

"But – 'kid' is a general term for a young person. I didn't know you were really a kid." She sighed. "That's so sad. You're so young, and…pitiful."

"So now you feel sorry for me. If I could hold a good fight with you for an hour I can't be that pitiful." The last thing I wanted was her pity.

"You're overly sensitive."

"You're overly rude."

"You're going to cry, aren't you?"

"What is wrong with you? What did I ever do to you? Why are you torturing me?"

"I'm not torturing you."

"Yes, you are."

"No, I just have an abrasive personality."

"So you make everyone you meet feel like dirt? You don't even know my name, and you hate me."

"I...I don't hate you."

"I couldn't tell." I rubbed a hand over my face. "I can't say anything without you jumping on my back, so I guess I'll just shut up." I laid down again.

"I wasn't fighting with you."

I didn't say anything. We stayed in painful silence for a long time.

"You look dead," Dana said finally.

"Don't go there."

She sighed. "We'll never get along, will we?"

I shook my head.

"Can I at least know your name?" That was as close to an apology as she was getting.

I guessed I'd have to forgive her. If I did, her words wouldn't hurt as much. "It's Rick," I said.

I heard her get up and walk away. The sounds of her footsteps in the grass disappeared. I supposed that meant she had put the argument behind her, and I guessed I would have to get over it, too.

When I thought about it, I realized that her being mean hadn't made me near as upset as when she'd pitied me. If she felt sorry for me that meant there was something wrong with me. I guessed if people felt sorry for me I would have to tell myself they didn't know any better. After all, I even felt sorry for myself sometimes. Although, when I remembered Jane's fiery little speech to me, it put things in perspective and I knew I'd gotten off well. No matter what people (or I) thought of me, I resolved to go through life without bitterness. It would be hard, but bitterness at everyone, including God, would just make me hateful like Dana. *Hey God, you can help out with the bitterness thing, can't you?* Somehow, I knew he would.

Chapter 7

I waited for Dana or the group to come back, whoever got to me first. I almost fell asleep. It was extremely boring.

Suddenly there was a chilling scream. I thought I had dozed off and imagined it, when the scream sounded again. I jumped to my feet, and realized there was nothing I could do to see who or what was making that noise. It screamed again, and this time I was sure it was human. I reached in the grass and grabbed my walking stick. If there was something dangerous out there, the most I could do to protect myself was whack it to death.

As the person screamed again, I thought maybe they needed help. Maybe Dana fell down the ravine and broke something. What could I do then? I could at least try and find the area where the group was and call them.

Indecision reigned in my brain. If I went towards the screaming, I could find the person to help them or be eaten by whatever was making them scream. My chances of being eaten were just as bad if I was standing here, so I hobbled off towards the screaming. I used my stick to determine whether I would run into anything. I held it just above the ground and waved it around a little. Thanks to my stick, I missed five trees and a small bush.

Judging by the direction of the screams, and vaguely recalling Jane's descriptions of the area, I was moving towards the forest to the right of the caves.

Getting through the actual forest was a nightmare. I scratched myself up, but since the screaming continued, I pursued it valiantly. As I got closer, I could make out what the person was saying.

"Help! Somebody please help me!"

"Hello?" I called. "Hello?" I crashed through a bush and halted.

"Rick?" It was Dana.

"What happened?" I panted.

"Rick?" Her shock was evident. "How did you get here?"

"Never mind. What's the matter?"

I heard her sniff, like she had been crying. "Um, he's hurt."

Oh, great, I thought, *she found an injured rabbit or something. And I had to go be the hero.* "Where'd you find it?" I wheezed.

"It?" she huffed. "He's a he. He's a man, stupid. It's the doctor."

"Colin?" I dropped to my knees and scooted towards her. "What happened?"

"I was walking through the woods, and I found him crawling along, trying to find help. His leg is injured. He could hardly talk. He was going to pass out and he said not to leave him, to press on the wound and just call for help. Then, he blacked out." She swallowed a sob.

"Oh, boy." I ran an arm across my damp forehead and tried to think. *What in the world happened to Colin? And where's the rest of the hunting party?* "Okay," I said finally, "you show me where to press, and then I'll stay with him while you go get the others."

"Alright."

She guided my hands to Colin's thigh. I pressed down with all my might and grimaced as something sticky oozed over my hand.

"You okay?" she asked.

"I got it. Go." I heard her run. I waited for a long time. I prayed over and over, *Don't let him die, don't let him die.* I didn't know him very well, but then again, I didn't know anyone on the island very well. Yet, there was something about surviving a catastrophe with someone that created a bond. And, Colin had saved my life, in a way, twice.

That reminded me of the alcohol he'd poured on my cut to sterilize it. There was no sign of help yet, and I didn't know how long they'd be. *A doctor would carry a bottle of that around, wouldn't he? Especially on something as accident-opportune as a hunt.* I reached into his pocket with one hand while keeping pressure on his leg with the other. "Jackpot!" I pulled out the bottle and unscrewed the cap with my teeth. Careful not to spill it all, I poured some into the wound. Setting the bottle aside, I wriggled out of my shirt. I tried holding it in my teeth and tearing it with my hand, but shirts only rip easily in movies. *Duh. What else would he carry to hunt?* I searched his belt and found a knife. A very sharp knife. Being extra careful not to gash myself, with one hand, and occasionally helping with my teeth, I cut my shirt into strips. I tied the strips together tightly, and wrapped it around Colin's leg. I knotted it and pulled as tight as I could, then knotted it again. I hoped I was doing the right thing. It was just instinctive. I kept pressure on it just in case, but I figured the cloth would help stop the bleeding.

What seemed an eternity later, I heard someone come crashing through the forest. "Rick!" It was Jane. I was never so happy to hear that voice.

"Thank God," I sighed. "Can you do something for him?"

"Let me see."

I sat back and just then realized I had no shirt on. Perfect. I'm stuck with no shirt again. I crossed my arms.

"Did you do this?" Jane asked. "The bandage?"

"Yeah."

"Good job. Let's see what I can do."

How does she know First Aid? It struck me as odd that she was the one to come to the rescue. She was an insurance saleswoman, after all. "Is he okay?"

"I think so." Her voice was shaky. "What could have happened to him? He's cut up pretty bad."

I shrugged. "What I wonder is, where's the rest of the hunting party?"

She didn't answer. I heard her doing something, shuffling around, but I didn't ask what it was.

"Where are the others?" I said.

"Grant and Darby were right behind me."

As if on cue, the two mentioned came up. "How is he?" Grant asked.

"He'll be okay," said Jane. "Grant, can you hand me your water bottle?"

Darby swore. "What happened to him?"

"Don't know," said Grant. "Dana said he didn't tell her."

"What happened to *you?*" Darby asked.

"Who, me?" I said.

"You're scratched up."

"Oh. I was running, and...it's nothing. Where's the rest of the group?"

"They stayed behind. We found some of the luggage."

We stood in silence a while. I didn't know exactly what was going on. The scrapes on my arms began to sting. I hoped I hadn't stepped in any poison ivy. Then I wondered whether poison ivy grew on a Pacific island.

I heard someone cough and moan. It turned out to be Colin, who was finally coming around.

"What...happened?" he said weakly.

I heard everybody sigh with relief, like we'd been holding our breath until he woke up.

"That's what we want to know," Grant answered him.

"How do you feel?" asked Jane. I wondered why everyone asked an injured person that.

"That's a stupid question," Colin said wryly, echoing my thoughts. "I feel terrible."

"What happened to you?" Grant asked.

"Oh, dear God..." Colin groaned. "They...came out of nowhere. We couldn't do anyfing. We tried to run, but it was too late. I made it this far. Have you found any of the others?"

"Just you."

"I hope they made it."

"Colin," said Grant, "who came after you? Who did this to you?"

"I couldn't see them," Colin sighed. "They shot from behind trees."

"What did they shoot you with?"

"Arrows."

"Where were you?"

"At the edge of this forest, beyond the mountain range. We'd bagged a good amount of meat and were headed back to camp."

"Here, drink this," said Jane. Her voice wasn't as strong as usual, but it wasn't the schoolgirl voice. This was more...compassionate.

Colin started to talk again, but they told him to save his strength.

I heard two people walk by me. Grant and Darby started talking in low voices, away from Colin. "Is he delirious?" mused Grant.

"I don't know," said Darby thoughtfully. "I don't think so. Should we wait to carry him back?"

"We won't make it all the way back to camp. We could at least get him to the cave before dark."

"Should we tell the others what he said?"

"No. There's no reason to scare them."

If there was someone out there shooting people, I thought, I would want to know.

Jane explained that Grant and Darby formed a chair with their arms and carried the top half of Colin while she and I carried his legs. Colin obliged to hold my walking stick.

The going was tough, and the wind was coming on strong. We finally got to the cave, where the rest of our group was waiting for us with a warm fire.

We got Colin situated and then ate the snack we'd brought with us.

Grant sat next to me as I finished off my fruit. "That was smart, you putting on the bandage."

"I saw it in a movie," I said with a smile. I shivered.

"Here." He handed me something. "Karen, Zack, Paul and Dana stayed behind to finish bringing the first load of luggage down here. You looked cold. I thought you might like a sweater since your shirt is in shreds."

"Thanks." I hadn't expected something like this from him. I pulled the sweater over my head and wrapped my arms around myself.

"You know, if you hadn't heard Dana call for help and gone crashing through the forest, Colin might not have made it. People underestimate others with disabilities a lot."

I tried not to show my surprise. Is he actually being human? "Do people underestimate you?" I asked slowly.

"Yeah. The others weren't so sure when I said I'd lead them up the cliff. They were thinking, 'How's he going to get up there using one hand?' I rock climb a lot, actually. I have since I was a kid, and after I recovered from the car accident, I learned how to climb again."

"Just like I'll learn to do certain things again."

"It's not as hard as it seems."

We sat quietly for a while, knowing we'd sort of made friends with each other. Finally, I decided to ask him what had been on my mind for some time. "Grant, why did you bring me along? Do you seriously think the transmitter is lost somewhere?"

"I like to look at all the possibilities. Although I get the feeling you disagree."

"I don't know. I just think it's impossible for the transmitter to have fallen out of the plane. It's kept in a compartment."

"Well...now I'm beginning to agree with you." He cleared his throat "We, uh, found something strange when we got to the luggage. All the bags had been searched before we got there. Paul and Karen had already found their bags on the beach, and some things were still on the plane, but the rest of our luggage was on the cliff. And things were missing. Strange things. CD players, book-lights, travel clocks, electronic toothbrushes, iPods, palm pilots, anything electric that didn't need to be plugged in."

I frowned. "Weird. Why would anyone take that kind of stuff?"

Grant sighed. "I can't figure it out."

"Does anybody besides us and Jane know about the flap in the plane?"

"Darby. He sort of over-heard Jane and I talking and demanded to know what was going on."

"That sounds like Darby."

"Anyway, we're thinking of leaving some people here to keep an eye on the luggage in case our thief comes back. You know what's odd? There were bags with money inside left behind."

I gulped audibly. "Then we're really dealing with a psycho."

I didn't sleep very well that night. Laying on rock didn't help the situation. I tried praying instead. *God, keep us safe from the weirdo running around. And whoever is shooting people.*

"What are you doing?" someone whispered hoarsely.

I jumped. "Who-"

"It's Jane. I'm staying awake to watch over Colin. I saw your lips moving."

"Um...I was just praying." It sounded awkward.

"Are you religious?"

"No. I believe in God. There's a difference."

"Really? Do you believe in Jesus and the death and resurrection and everything?"

"Yeah, I do. I accepted salvation a long time ago, but I sort of forgot about it until the plane crash. It kind of put things in perspective."

"Oh. My family was Catholic. I guess I couldn't handle the religious stuff any more."

"You don't have to be religious. My family was sort of revolutionary, I guess. We didn't even go to church. We just figured the only important thing was to maintain a relationship with God. And I just pray in my head. I figure if God's listening, I just have to talk, like I would talk to you. As long as I have him watching over me, it's easier to not be afraid. In the end, whatever he decides will happen, will happen."

"Is that why you're so...confident?"

"Yeah, I guess."

"I wish I was as confident."

"You could be."

She laughed quietly. "I'm still thinking about it."

I nodded understandingly. There was no reason to push her. "How's Colin?"

"He'll be okay." She yawned.

"Look, I can't sleep. I'll stay with Colin and if I hear something, I'll wake you up."

"Really? Would you? Oh, thank you so much."

I stayed up for quite some time. Eventually, the expected rain fell. After a few hours, Colin started to stir. "Rick?" he said hoarsely.

"Yeah. You okay?"

"Yeah." I heard him let out a deep breath. "I'm worried about the rest of the hunting group."

"They'll turn up," I said hopefully.

He laughed. "Are you being optimistic?"

"Why?"

"Oh, you have no idea what it was like. It's hard for me to believe they made it. It's a miracle I made it."

"So…have I got this straight? You were coming back to camp with food, and all of a sudden something or someone started shooting arrows at you. You ran. You got separated from the group. Dana found you."

"That's it."

"When did you get shot at?"

"It would have been – assuming it's past midnight right now - yesterday morning."

"And we found you yesterday evening. You crawled around, wounded, a long time. Thank goodness Dana was senseless enough to walk into the forest by herself."

"Yeah. How exactly did you find her?"

"She screamed like a banshee. I thought she was dying or something and I crashed through the forest like a madman to help. I finally found her."

"I see. How are you?"

"I'm cold and hungry and I'm full of nettle stings, or whatever the Pacific equivalent of nettles is, but I think I'll live."

"No. I mean about not seeing."

"Oh, that. I deal with it. It's scary sometimes. And it's painful. I really, really wish it hadn't happened. But it's not as terrible as I thought it would be at first. I mean, I'm alive. My heart is beating, my limbs are in place, and I'm talking to you. And I wasn't the one who got shot by mysterious persons and given First Aid by someone who didn't know what he was doing."

Colin laughed again. "I guess you're okay."

"Yeah. At least, I know I will be."

"Good." I heard him shift his position a little. After a while I heard him breathing deeply, and knew he was asleep. I rubbed my sore behind and tried to think of something to keep myself awake. I leaned my head against the cold cave wall and my eyelids drooped shut.

Chapter 8

"Rick."

My head snapped up. With agony, I realized I had fallen asleep. I rubbed my face. "Sorry," I said groggily.

"It's okay," Jane laughed. "It's morning."

"Oh. How's Colin?"

"He's still asleep. He'll be fine, though."

"Jane, how do you know about all this, um, doctor stuff? I mean, you're an insurance lady."

"I took nursing classes for a while in college," she explained. "Found out nursing wasn't my thing."

"Maybe you were wrong."

It had stopped raining for the time being. After a breakfast consisting of fruit from someone's backpack, it was decided who would bring the first load of luggage to camp and who would stay behind. Dana had found her bag and wanted to go back to camp. She, Karen, Zack and Paul offered to carry the luggage and the bags of water bottles. Paul told me they had brought a tarp from camp, and by using poles through the two ends of the tarp, they could pile the luggage inside and carry the poles across their shoulders.

I was going to stay behind in the cave to be with Colin while Darby, Grant, and Jane went back to the cliff to sort through the remaining luggage.

It was a long day, and in the middle of it, it started raining again. The rain fell lightly, but I knew the group on top of the cliff would be soaked. It had been a long time since I'd seen rain, and I couldn't see it now, but I could smell it and hear it and feel it. I could even taste it. I went to the edge of the cave and stuck out my hand. The rain felt good. I opened my mouth. The cold drops plopped onto my tongue.

When I was a kid, and we still lived in the Chicago suburbs, my dad and I would sometimes go down to the creek right after it rained and play with little toy boats. We pretended they were trapped in a storm. We would use little army figurines to be the passengers. It was especially fun to trap the figurines in the mud. Noah was twelve years older than me, so he didn't play as much, but it was more fun when he did. We didn't care if we were soaked and dirty – in fact, that made it even better.

My mother, of course, wasn't exactly thrilled when we did this, but they were experiences we wouldn't forget. So, she stood on our porch and waved to us and smiled.

After Mom and Dad died and I got older, I lost all interest in going out in the rain. I disliked being wet, as most older people do. But I still enjoyed the memories of playing boats in a muddy creek.

Tropical rain smelled and tasted different than Chicago rain. I suddenly missed my old home very much. I even missed Noah's fancy apartment. I even slightly missed Aunt Sandy and her husband Mike's place. I didn't know where home would be any more. *Will I go back to living with Aunt Sandy and Uncle Mike? Will they want to take care of me? I was in the way when I was a normal kid – what are they going to do with me now? Maybe mom's friend Sharon will take me.* I sighed and realized I didn't have to worry about all that right now. Paul was right - I agonized over things too much. Right now I just had to worry about being eaten by cannibals with arrows and attacked by psychos with travel clocks. I tilted my head back and laughed, because things kept happening that I wouldn't have believed were possible if someone had told me about them.

"What're you doing?" Colin called.

I shook my head and turned to face his direction. "I'm just going crazy."

"Oh. That's all." He groaned. "My leg hurts like-" He paused. "Like heck," he finished.

I went and sat by him. "In movies, the doctor never gets hurt."

"I don't count. I'm an intern."

"Why were you going to America?"

"Doctor's conference."

I rubbed my finger in the dirt.

"You look bored."

"Very observant of you. There isn't much to do." I sighed. "Colin – is that your first name?"

"Yeah. Colin Westley."

"'Dr. Westley.' That's very British. Was your dad a doctor, too?"

"No. I didn't know 'im very well. He divorced my mum when I was a kid. My mum was a doctor. She was a good one, too."

"Did she die?"

"No. She's retired. She's not planning to leave this world for a while yet. It gave her troubles, and she's going to give everybody a hard time as long as she can."

"She sounds nice."

"She's annoying, but I love her. What does your dad do?"

"He used to be an architect and carpenter. He taught me about both of those jobs. My mom and dad are dead."

"And your brother, too? Life has been rough on you."

"But I'm still here." At that moment, I heard voices coming towards us. "Sounds like they're tired of being wet and are coming back."

"Wimps," Colin murmured.

The group came into the cave, making quite a racket.

Suddenly Colin shouted "Professor!"

"I'm glad they found you, Doctor," said Professor Taylor, the chemistry teacher. I was as surprised to hear him as Colin was to see him. "You can't know my elation to have seen your companions on the cliff up there."

"What happened?" Colin asked.

"I escaped with only a scratch," started the professor breathlessly, "but I'm afraid the rest of our group didn't fare so well. After I knew it was safe, I went back and found their bodies. Then I tried to find you. I went north. When I reached the edge of the forest, I was met by the sea. So I followed the beach slightly east. I was behind the mountain range we can see from our camp. And I saw a mountain that stands behind the range. Its peak is very high, and there's something at the top of it. And I saw several plumes of smoke coming from its base. There's obviously a camp there. The people who shot us must live there."

"That means Rick was right," said Jane. "There are natives of this island living here."

I felt gratified that she mentioned me.

The professor continued. "I thought it best to get away from that area. So I retraced my steps, and that's when I found these three on the cliff."

"So what does all this native stuff mean for us?" Darby asked.

"It means we might as well be dead," Colin said matter-of-factly.

"Wait a minute," said Grant, ever the optimist, "all of us survivors might outnumber them. And they might be afraid to approach us."

"They sure weren't afraid when they shot us," Colin pointed out.

"I think…" said Jane slowly, "that as long as we stay far away from them, we'll be safe. The hunting group was probably using the natives' hunting grounds, and the natives weren't happy about it."

"You may be right," began Grant. "However, it might be better to approach them and try and work out some kind of peace treaty."

"You're a blasted idiot if you try that," said Colin.

"Why?"

"Because they have weapons! They'll slaughter us. What're you going to do? Walk out to the mountain wif a little white flag and say 'Hey! We come in peace! Take us to your leader!'"

That presented a funny picture, and it was the sort of thing Grant would do. I held back a laugh.

"Rick, is something funny?"

"Look, we argue a lot. We speculate a lot." I shrugged. "It's not getting us anywhere. My grandpa used to say if all people were mutes things would get done much faster. There's nothing we can do about the natives. I say we go on like we have been, trying to survive while we wait for a rescue team, but stay away from the natives, like Jane said." I just then realized I was a fourteen-year-old kid telling a bunch of adults what was best for them. On the other hand, they were silly adults.

"Rick is right," Colin said.

"Rick is usually right," Jane added.

"'Out of the mouths of babes,'" muttered Darby.

Grant didn't seem too happy to be outdone by a little boy. "Okay, we'll avoid them. But how are we going to eat if we can't hunt in their territory?"

"There must be other places to hunt game," put in Professor Taylor. "All we need to do is explore the island."

"And what if we run into the natives again?" Darby asked.

"We'll stay on this side of the mountain range."

"Who should we send to explore it?"

Grant answered that. "Well, Colin couldn't make it."

"I could so," Colin argued. "Give me a big stick to lean on and a day or so and I could."

"That's not a good idea," Jane said quickly. "You're just being stubborn. You're really injured."

"I'm not injured that bad. And what if one of you gets hurt? All the medical supplies are at the beach. I would know how to compromise wifout them."

"What about the people that were hurt in the crash?" she countered.

"They're being taken care of," Colin assured her.

"If the doctor says he can go, he can," said the Professor. "You can't really stop him."

"Alright," Grant relented. "And I think the professor and the group we had to get the luggage should go – minus one or two people."

"Like me," I said. I suddenly wanted to go with them. "But if you find a radio or something, it's your fault I'm not there." I was using the Airplane Boy technique.

There was a moment of hesitation. "I think you'd better come along," Grant said after a while.

Score one for Airplane Boy. I didn't know why I wanted to explore the island with them. Maybe because I knew if I stayed in camp I would have nothing to do but feel sorry for myself. But thanks to Grant's weird way of thinking, I was going with them.

Later on, Jane dropped something heavy beside me. "Almost forgot," she said. "We found these two bags, along with the co-pilot's, down by the edge of the cliff today. One is yours, one is your brother's."

"Thanks." It was unexpected, to actually have my stuff back. I'd given up hope of finding it. "Which one is mine?"

"The one closest to you. I'll see you later."

"Okay." I pulled my bag towards me and unzipped it. My iPod, as was expected, was missing. I couldn't remember everything in my bag, but I figured the rest was all there. In the bottom I had a small picture album with family pictures. I hadn't wanted to leave it at Aunt Sandy's. It was too important to me. The pictures wouldn't do me much good now, but I was glad I still had them. When our old house was sold, after Mom and Dad died, I had to get rid of most of my stuff to move into Aunt Sandy's. I wasn't happy to see all of it go. My most prized possessions that remained were the picture album, some of my mom's jewelry, and three army figurines my dad made out of wood. Noah got all of Dad's tools, which he saved and put in storage. I was glad we didn't have to sell them, and glad Noah appreciated them enough to keep them. What was an airplane pilot going to do with carpentry tools, after all? He said when I was older I could have them. He knew I wanted to be a carpenter. He said I would be good at it. He said it was all about my seeing the details.

As I thought about it, I choked up. I buried my face in my arms and leaned on my knees. I counted to ten and refused to cry. I'd gone through this before when Mom and Dad died. In school, kids would look at me funny and feel sorry for me. Or, Aunt Sandy would mention something like, *"You look the very picture of the two of them"* at the dinner table. Odd things like that would set me off. Some people believe boys never cry. I did. Only a few times, but I did. I felt better as time went on. But then the airplane crash happened and I couldn't take that without letting some of the pain out.

That part of the emotional process was over. Now I'd just have little, once-in-a-while times when I'd remember something and it would hurt for a while. I was afraid, just a little bit, that something might happen to set me off and I would go ballistic on someone. That I might reach a point where all the frustration and confusion would explode out of me. But for the time being, I'd set my feelings aside and worry about keeping up with the rest of the group on the hike. And, of course, avoid being shot or eaten or burned at the stake or whatever natives really did.

Chapter 9

Day Nine, the next day, the rest of our group (minus Dana, who complained of sore feet) came back to get the rest of the luggage. They volunteered to help explore, but we had to get the rest of the luggage to camp first. Besides, we all knew Colin could use another day off his leg. Grant, Jane and Darby took their turn to haul the luggage while the rest of us stayed put. Paul and I took guesses on who would be voted off the island first if this was Survivor. Paul said Dana. At first, jokingly, I said Grant if he didn't watch it. Then I picked Dana.

The next day, Grant, Jane and Darby came back with some rather over-ripe fruit to eat. We found a walking stick for Colin, and Paul smoothed it with his knife a little, like he did my stick. I remembered, sadly, that I used to be able to carve.

Everyone took a small backpack with some supplies (no one specified to me what exactly 'supplies' were), some fruit, and extra clothes. I changed out of the sweater and into one of my shirts from my luggage.

We set out towards the east, through the fields. Colin and I sort of hung in the back by each other, and he cussed most of the journey. I said at least we could thank God Grant didn't have us tied together again. He said he'd thank God when he was off this island. Colin wasn't the complaining type, and I knew he was probably rethinking walking on his hurt leg. But, he also wasn't the sort to back down.

We walked across what seemed like an endless stretch of nothing, with, I was told, mountains on our left and more grass on our right. I remembered taking a field trip to a farm, back in Illinois. We'd walked across an empty field to get to a pumpkin patch. The pumpkins were for souvenirs. We ended up with souvenirs much worse – blisters and sunburn. Walking across the fields now, I wished I had some of Dana's suntan lotion.

"I'm an idiot," Colin huffed to himself. "Hey, you look overheated."

"I am. I'm from the Windy City. I hate heat like this."

"I'm from Norfern England. This is killing me, too."

I seriously doubted he could be as hot I was. "Where'd we get these backpacks?" I asked as we marched on.

"Jane collected them from the passengers or somefing…" His voice trailed off.

"I'll only say this once," I ventured. "Are you sure you should keep walking?"

"I can make it."

"Okay. Colin, what exactly are we hunting with?"

"Everyfing. A couple of guys that had been hunting in England – they're the ones I went hunting wif when we were shot - had a gun case on board, and a few knife cases. Even a crossbow. Rope for traps. All that. And another passenger had a 9mm, also locked up."

"We had an entire arsenal on board." I was glad we had the weapons and the psycho did not - if there was a psycho. "Isn't it kind of weird to have that many weapons on an airplane?"

"The hunters had to get permits and special permission to even have it, and their weapons were kept in a sealed trunk to which only the air marshal had a key. But the trunk got damaged in the crash and we popped it open. As for the other gun, we're not sure whose it was. We smashed that case open."

The air grew hotter and slightly sticky as the day wore on. Towards evening, someone shot something, but Colin and I were too far back from the group to determine much more. When we caught up and helped make camp we were still in the fields. It turned out that they had shot a rabbit, which we cooked and ate. Meat tasted so heavenly after all that stupid fruit.

I took my shoes and socks off and wiggled my toes. Paul came to sit beside me. "Long day, Dude."

"Yup."

"You've got sunburn or somethin'. Your face is red."

"Perfect."

"I think everybody's sunburned." He sighed. "Were you always like that?"

"Like what?"

"Cynical. You know, like, serious."

"My life's not exactly a fairy tale."

Paul was quiet for a while. "What does that mean...?"

I considered. "No, I wasn't always like that. After Mom and Dad died, I guess is when it happened. I never noticed it until I started traveling with Noah. He was more of a kid than I was."

"You miss him a lot." It was a statement, not a question.

"Yeah, I do. But truthfully, I didn't know him that well. He was born when my parents first got married. I don't know why they waited twelve years to have me. I guess Mom wanted a baby again. Anyway, Noah was a lot older. When I was seven he went away to college. I got to know him better after I started traveling with him, but there was always a gap of years between us that we couldn't quite get over. Still, he was my best friend. He was my brother, after all."

"My brother died when I was eight."

I was surprised. "You never mentioned a brother."

"He was my little brother," Paul said quietly. "He died of leukemia. He was only six. His death broke my mom's heart."

"Wow." I rubbed my stinging arms. "Did your mom ever get over it?"

"Yeah, actually. She learned to move on. I always wondered what Silas would be like if he'd lived, though."

I supposed that was why Paul wanted to be my friend; taking care of me was like taking care of his little brother. "Did you say your brother's name was Silas? You guys were 'Paul and Silas,' like in the Bible story?"

He laughed. "My mom's idea. It was pretty cool. Mom's a, like, Bible freak. She quotes verses in her sleep, I swear."

"Are you a Christian?"

"Totally. And you?"

"Also totally."

"That so rocks. It's an awesome experience, is it not?"

"Totally," I laughed.

"Does it help with the...you know, with being blind and your family dying?"

"Yeah. It helps to know I'm being watched over, and that there's a bigger purpose in life. Even if I really don't understand what that purpose is."

"Cool."

"I guess." I nodded. "Totally."

Our group hiked another day across fields. I got to know Zach and Karen a little better by catching pieces of their conversation. They were friends from L.A. who were sports maniacs. They went to England to try and swim the Channel. Apparently their sponsors bailed out at the last minute and the two were headed back home when we crashed.

By the end of that day the group said the mountain range was ending and they saw a forest ahead. We set up camp for the night and looked forward to a more eventful day.

Everyone was tired and a little grumpy. Grant decided to make it worse. "Okay, guys," he began in his Announcement Voice.

We all groaned.

"Can we leave off the Nobel speech tonight?" yawned Darby.

I heard Zach snicker.

Grant sniffed and clicked his tongue. "Oh, sure, sure. I get it. You've brought me out here to no-man's land to mutiny, is that it?" His voice was harsh. I didn't think he was exactly joking.

Darby must not have recognized Grant's tone. "What are you going to tell us? 'Good job boys and girls,'" he said in a patronizing voice, "'now go to sleepy and we'll go explore the forest in the morning. And, oh, don't worry about the big bad men trying to kill us, because I'll protect you with my magic sword.'"

"Darby, what exactly is your problem?" I was surprised to hear Colin say in a low voice.

"My problem is someone who thinks we're still in the real world. Someone who acts like we're getting out of here any minute now. We're not."

"So what do you want me to do?" said Grant. "Give up? Assume the worst? Okay." He was mad now, and I didn't blame him. "Okay, fine, Colin's in charge. I'll go back to camp and wait for the rescue plane and you guys go on into the dark unknown and build a tree-house, because obviously you'll be here for a very long time. Maybe I'll write you." I heard him pick up his pack and walk off.

"That was brilliant, mate," Colin muttered.

Darby snorted.

"Did you hear anything I said at the beach?" Jane said sharply. She got no answer. "Colin, you should talk to Grant," she said.

"He won't listen to me."

"You're in charge as much as he is."

"No, I'm not," Colin retorted. "You talk to him."

"He won't listen to me, either."

"Take Rick," Colin said. "You two together ought to do it."

Jane sighed heavily. Finally she grabbed my arm and dragged me along with her in search of Grant.

"This is stupid," she muttered. "They're adults, for crying out loud. Why do you and I always have to sort things out?"

"You have a point."

"Grant!" Jane shouted. "Grant, come back!" She let go of my arm and walked away. Obviously she had caught up with him. "Grant, don't listen to Darby. He's a spoiled brat." They were a few feet in front of me.

"Jane, I give up," Grant sighed.

I stepped forward uncertainly. "Somebody has to be in charge."

"Colin is in charge," Grant answered.

"Colin doesn't want to be in charge," Jane said.

"Why not?"

"I don't know. Just…come back. Please."

"It won't be any better at the beach," I said when Grant didn't answer. I couldn't tell if Jane and I were making any progress.

"It's useless," he said finally.

"What is?"

"This whole hike. We won't find the transmitter. All we've caught so far is a rabbit. And we can't survive without food any longer. I mean, look at us. We all look exhausted and starving."

"Thanks a lot," Jane murmured.

"No, I don't mean that. We're all going to start getting sick pretty soon, though, with lack of nutrition. What are we going to do? What am I going to do? I'm responsible for these people."

"Why?" I asked.

"Somebody has to be responsible. It happens to be me."

"But there's no point in you leaving the hike," Jane said. "Rick's right, it'll be worse for you at the beach. And we still might find more animals to hunt if we go on."

"I guess I got myself into this mess," Grant admitted. "I just didn't know it would be like this."

"No one did. Come back, Grant. We need you." She was very convincing.

"No, you don't. But I'll come back anyway."

"Good," Jane said. I could tell she was smiling.

"Boy," Grant said tiredly. "I was only on that plane because some rogue agent messed things up. All I had to do was apologize to England and go home to a three-week vacation. Now I'm stuck on an island with – Jane, why are you looking at me like that?"

"Like what?" Jane said flatly.

"Nothing," Grant sighed. "I'm just edgy. Sorry."

"Yeah," she said. She cleared her throat. "Let's go," she said in a normal voice.

Grant was welcomed back by the others, excluding Darby, who had walked off somewhere to be angry.

"What does Darby look like?" I asked Paul.

"An English brat. Spiky black hair, dark clothes. Just normal enough to be under the radar and punk enough to prove he has attitude. He's, like, weird."

"It seems to me," I mused, "that in an emergency situation when he has to take control he's okay. But when someone else can take care of him he's a jerk."

"Dude," Paul laughed.

"What?"

"You should be a shrink, man. It's paid cynicism. Fits you great."

I reached over and shoved him.

"Dude," he said in a shocked voice.

"What now?"

"You pushed me, man. How'd you know where I was?"

I paused. "I can smell you and feel you, like your body heat or whatever. I can hear that your voice is close, too. Wow." I rubbed the back of my neck. "I guess I'm good at second sight."

"You're brave, that's it. You got over the pity party and taught yourself to do stuff. If I were you I'd sit in a corner and feel sorry for myself."

"I might have done that if Grant hadn't said I could come."

"You're cool."

I smiled. "I try my best."

We went through the forest on Day Eleven. It took a long, frustrating time. The undergrowth wrapped itself around our legs. We accidentally spread out from each other, trying to find a clear path. I got stuck in a bunch of mean weeds. I tried to untangle myself, but I tripped and got stuck further.

I somehow managed to get my arms tied together. I panicked and I tried to hear the others to determine how far behind I was.

"I guess you want help," called Darby. I was actually relieved to hear him. "You've really screwed up."

"Thanks," I panted. I wiped sweat from my forehead.

He stumbled up and tried to untangle me.

"So…what's your story?" I attempted a casual conversation, which was pretty silly considering the situation I was in.

"I'm an upper-crust little monster from London," he answered. "My parents tried to get me to be a good boy, but I like partying. They shipped me off to University, but I still hung out with a crowd they didn't like and partied all night.

Got in trouble a lot, but my dad's a big wheel, so the school couldn't do much to me. I made it to graduation. Then I was out late one night and I busted up my dad's car. That was the last straw. They were shipping me off to the States to my uncle to give me a job and to get me away from my friends. Iowa," he laughed. "They were sending me to Iowa. I hate them." He snapped a vine loose.

"Well, an island does a lot for anger management," I said. "You can yell and scream at people as long as you want, and no one can stop you."

"That's juvenile," he scoffed. Then he paused as he realized what I was getting at. "You're saying that's what I've been doing."

"Haven't you?"

He pulled more vines apart. They made a popping noise. "Why do you say insightful things like that? Shouldn't a kid like you be back on the beach swimming or playing with fire or something?"

"Yeah, all blind kids should play with fire."

He pulled a vine off my arm. I winced. He unwrapped another one from my leg. "What is this stuff?" he mumbled. He yanked one off my wrist.

"Ow! Geez!" My eyes watered.

"You okay?" he asked, almost concerned. "This is some kind of weird island thing…it's wrapping around me now." He swore. "I'm stuck. Now what?"

Chapter 10

We sat around in embarrassed silence until who but Jane should come to the rescue.

"Are you guys okay?" she asked. "We couldn't see you, so I came back." Suddenly she started laughing. "You look really miserable."

I was glad to hear her laugh, but not exactly in the mood to join her. Between the three of us we got Darby and I and my walking stick unwrapped. Darby and I left the area as quickly as possible. We joined the others, who were standing in a clearing.

"How much longer do you think we have to hike through this forest?" Jane asked. "I'd say we've already gone about a mile."

"I agree," said Grant. "I can't tell how much forest is left-"

"If you'll permit me to be blunt," interjected the Professor, "we are not in a forest, but a jungle."

"Okay, I don't know how much jungle is left."

"The odd thing," continued the Professor, "is that this area of jungle is different from the one in which we hunted before. You may remember, Dr. Westley, of my telling you of the odd plants I found."

"What odd plants?" asked Grant.

"Plants that would not naturally be found in a tropic environment," answered Professor Taylor. "I would say that these particular plants were native of Europe."

"What are you saying?" asked Darby.

"I'm saying that someone planted European plants on a tropical island."

I imagined everyone was staring at each other in a confused way.

"But this part of the island's forest – jungle – we're in now has no European plants?" clarified Grant.

"Correct," answered the Professor.

"Is this important?" said Darby bluntly.

The Professor tsked. "Everything is important in some way."

Darby laughed. "Uh-huh."

"Thank you for your...informative speech, Prof. Taylor. We're still going west," said Grant, guiding the subject back to the hike. "Perhaps we should try going north now."

"Why?"

"Look," sighed Grant, "We're not making any progress. I say some of us continue west, some go north, some go south. How does that sound?"

Everyone agreed.

"Now, there are nine of us. We'll split into threes. I'll lead a group, Colin will lead a-"

"Why do any of us have to lead?" asked Colin. "There'll only be three of us in a group."

"Good point. Uh...how'll we decide who goes with who?"

"'Bubble gum,'" said Zach.

"Excuse me?"

"You know, 'Bubble gum, bubble gum, in a dish...' We use that to pick partners on hikes."

"I – I don't know what you're talking about," said Grant confusedly.

"Okay, put your foot in," said Karen.

Somehow we worked it out. I felt sorry for diplomatic Grant, whose fate was determined by a children's rhyme.

The teams were Jane, Colin and I to continue west, Grant, Zach, and Karen to go north, Darby, Prof. Taylor and Paul to go south. Before we split up, we agreed to meet back at our last campsite outside of the woods in twenty-four hours.

I felt a lot less safe from natives with only Colin and Jane, and I wished I could have gone with Paul. I was tired, too, and I kept tripping over things as the three of us headed west. Colin and Jane talked. I concentrated on staying upright.

"Where are you from?" Colin asked Jane.

"L.A. You?"

"You've never heard of it. It's up in Norfern England. What do you do?"

"I'm an insurance salesperson."

"Really? What's your full name?"

"Jane Redford."

"Sounds more like an actress than a salesperson."

"When I was little I wanted to be an actress," she said sheepishly.

"When I was little I wanted to be a truck driver."

Jane laughed. "What made you decide to be a doctor?"

"Ambition. My mum's ambition. She worked frough medical school, and then she was a renowned doctor. She wanted me to be like her."

"How do you like being like your mother?"

"It's good. I guess. It pays enough that I don't have to like it. It's hard to meet people. You know, girls. I don't have time to date. Do you have a boyfriend?"

She paused. "Are you hitting on me?"

"No," he laughed.

"Good. Because you remind me of my brother."

Ouch, I thought. Poor Colin. I know how you feel, buddy. Why does she do that? Is that the only line she knows? How about 'Back off, buster!' or, 'Talk to the hand!' At least you'd know you were being insulted.

"So do you have a boyfriend?" persisted Colin.

"Not now. I was engaged," she answered quietly. "A while ago...he died."

"Wow. I'm sorry. How?"

"He was murdered."

"Oh," he said abruptly.

No wonder she's melancholy.

The conversation turned to small talk for a while. I learned that when Colin was in medical school, he had a part-time job to help pay the bills. His mom would have paid it all, but he liked to contribute. I guessed it was a guy-esteem thing. Jane said she went to college to become an accountant. She ended up in the insurance racket later because of her experience with numbers. They talked about food they liked after that. Then it was movies. I chimed in once and a while, but I was getting more worn out by the minute. I could tell by the strain in their voices that they felt much the same.

I tripped over something and fell.

I heard them stop walking. "Rick, you okay?" asked Colin.

"I've been better," I said wryly.

"You want to rest a minute?"

Would that mean I'm weak? Would they realize they're dragging a little kid around? Do I care any more? "Just for a minute. I'm not used to all this walking."

"Good," said Colin. "I could use a rest, too." I heard them sit down.

"You've been pushing yourself pretty hard," Jane said to me. "You sure you aren't wearing yourself out?"

How should I answer that? "I'm sure." I was probably wearing myself out, but then again, we all were. We sat still for a while. I was worried I might fall asleep.

"Ready?" asked Colin after a while. "I'd like to get out of here before dark. Rick, are you going to be alright?"

I came very close to asking for a piggy-back ride. "I'll be fine."

We marched on. Just when I was seriously considering calling it quits, I heard something. Jane and Colin were talking about another common interest. It was good Jane was finally talking to someone, but I wasn't paying particular attention. And then I heard it - a roaring noise. I didn't have a clue what it was, and frankly, I wasn't in the mindset to consider it a friendly noise. "Guys! What is that?"

They stopped talking. "It sounds like...the ocean, maybe?" Colin's voice trailed off. "Maybe we're at the end of the forest."

We decided to go towards the noise. It got louder as we walked. I heard them quit walking, and as I caught up Jane grabbed my arm. "Why are we stopping?" I asked.

"We're at the end of the forest," Jane answered. "There's a steep embankment leading downwards, and then a huge rock formation. There must be a spring under the rock. From here it looks like there's a waterfall coming out of the middle of it. It's facing away from us, but I think it goes into a lake."

"Everyfing is very lush looking, isn't it?" Colin said.

"Wow," Jane breathed. "It's really pretty."

I tried to imagine what it looked like. "Can we get down there?"

Colin let out a long breath. "The hill to get down is mostly loose rock. We'll slide most of the way. Right, I'll go first."

I heard him and Jane slide down the embankment. I let my walking stick and backpack roll down, then I sat down with my feet planted on the edge of the embankment. "How far down is it?" I asked, suddenly worried I'd slip and crack my noggin.

"It's about a hundred feet long!" Jane shouted at me. "It's not too steep! Just slide, and we'll catch you!"

I was concerned about how far away she sounded. Before I got too scared, I pushed off. I tipped sideways about halfway down and rolled. They did indeed catch me at the bottom, but not until after I'd endured a very bumpy ride.

I sat on the grass a moment to catch my breath.

"You okay?" asked Colin.

I stood up and wiped dirt from my face. "When I was little, I fell off a slide once, at a park. My mom had to take me to the emergency room because I had gravel imbedded up my nose." I shook my pant leg and felt some pebbles slide out. "I guess I was never very good at sliding."

I heard Jane attempting to hold back a giggle. She was much happier since we split from the group. It seemed like letting us know her fiancé died had taken a load off her shoulders.

The three of us walked around. They kept making comments about how pretty it was. After a minute we stopped again.

"What are you doing?" I heard Jane say to Colin.

"I'm gettin' in that water and I'm not getting out for a long while," he answered happily. I heard a giant splash.

"I suppose that means we strip down to our boxers and jump in," I said wryly. I was already shirtless as it was, but somehow the image of me in swim trunks didn't present a Tommy Hillfinger magazine-cover picture.

"I wear my swimsuit under my clothes," Jane said practically. I heard her dive into the water. "C'mon, Rick, this is really nice!"

Oh, what the heck. I took off my jeans and walked to where I could feel the edge of the bank. Suddenly I was afraid again. My encounter while bathing in the ocean hadn't made my relationship with swimming any better.

"Rick, c'mon!" Jane called again.

"I can't," I said stiffly. "I can't swim."

I could tell by their sudden, uneasy silence they'd remembered who I was. On the hike I could hold my own, but now I was the little blind boy again, the boy who needed help.

So what's wrong with that? A sensible voice yelled in my head. What's so wrong with relying on people sometimes? You cut yourself off from people all the time. You never want to bother anyone. But what's so awful about asking for help, for something you need?

"Rick?" Jane got out of the water and stood next to me. "We can jump in together."

I reached out and grabbed her hand. "I'm scared," I said bluntly.

"You don't have to be."

"I'm on reserve, Rick!" Colin called from the water. "You can trust bof of us!"

"On three," Jane said. "One, two, three."

I jumped.

I prayed Jane wouldn't let go of my hand. I prayed I wouldn't drown like a rat. I prayed I would just trust Jane and Colin. For once I would rely on someone else to take care of me.

I thought of all of this in the few seconds that we went flying through the air. Right before we hit the water, I sucked in a breath. As we dropped below the surface, I held Jane's hand in a fierce grip. She never let go. She pulled me up to the surface. I breathed in and shook my head to get the water off my face. Then I started to sink. Colin grabbed my arm. "Can you float, mate?"

"No," I rasped. But who cares? Ever since I hit the water, I wasn't scared. I was so grateful that I had trusted them. I let out a little victory whoop. "Man, that was great. Now that I'm in the water, I only wish I could swim."

I never thought I'd learn to master swimming. And I never could have imagined I'd learn it without being able to see anything. But Jane and Colin insisted on teaching me how. In fact, Colin actually said, "We're not getting out of this lake until you can at least float."

I floated, all right, and dog-paddled, too. I drew the line at the breast-stroke. "Let me get used to this or you're going to kill me."

Jane had the amazing and rather odd foresight to bring little travel soap and shampoo bottles (confiscated from the luggage we'd found) in her bag. She shared, and all three of us scrubbed down before leaving the lake.

When we were out of the water, we used some t-shirts of Colin's to dry us off. I changed into a pair of cargo shorts and a fresh t-shirt. Then we sat under some trees and relaxed. I felt very clean. I could smell Jane's perfume. I wondered what kind of person wore perfume in the middle of nowhere. *Obviously a person who is the definition of, 'Always be prepared.'*

"This shampoo makes me smell girly, doesn't it?" Colin asked. "Here, Rick, smell my head."

I smelled his hair. "It does. Oh, great, that means mine does, too."

"You two are so guy-ish," Jane said.

"You mean 'manly?'" Colin suggested.

"No, I mean 'guy-ish.' There's a difference."

"Well, then," countered Colin, "you're very…'girly.'"

"I'm not girly."

"She's not girly," I said truthfully. Prepared, yes. Girly, no. Not Jane.

"I kick-box," said Jane. "That is *not* girly."

"*You* kick-box?" He was obviously surprised. "Why would an insurance saleswoman kick-box?"

She paused. "Why not? Rick, could you see me kickboxing?"

"I can see you doing a lot of surprising things, Jane."

"I suppose you have a secret life," Colin went on. "I suppose you're a spy or somefing."

"I wish," Jane laughed. I noticed it was the same laugh she used when she was doing the school-girl act. I was the only one who would have recognized that, though. I was always looking at the details no one noticed.

"You sure you're not a spy?" I said in a low tone.

"Oh, Rick, quit being so serious. She's no more a spy than you are."

"Maybe he is," Jane said.

"Sure, sure, I'm a spy. I've had you snowed all this time. I make James Bond look like a kindergartner."

"He jokes!" laughed Colin in a pompous voice. "Can you believe it, folks? Ol' Iceman jokes! Har har!"

Jane was actually giggling. It was her real laugh now, which made me extremely determined to find out why she kept hiding things behind her unassuming mask. She was much more fun when she stayed herself.

Chapter 11

We didn't have enough daylight to travel, so we set up camp and got ahead on our sleep.

The next day we followed the river across more of the lush valley, until it cut through raised ground, creating a gorge (Jane was most helpful in explaining this).

We climbed up the embankment and found that at the top the ground remained level. As we walked, the ground became sandier, until we were walking on a beach. I could hear the ocean, which sounded very close, and Jane eventually told me it surrounded the beach on two sides. Finally, we came to the end of the beach, which surprisingly also turned out to be the end of the island. Colin was whooping "We made it! We made it! Oh, yeah!" and Jane was giggling at him. I was wishing I was wearing suntan lotion again, and the wind coming off the sea kept whipping sand into my face.

"I guess this it," Jane said. "We go back now."

"It's too bad we have to re-join the group," Colin said as we turned back. "I liked just being wif you guys much better."

"I, uh…" Jane began slowly.

"Yes?" Colin prompted.

"I'd appreciate it if you guys didn't mention about my fiancé to the others. It's…you know…a private thing."

"Sure," Colin and I said quickly.

After a while, Colin said "I wonder if we could convince the ofers to stay in the valley we found for a while. You know, to get our strengf back. If we walk all the way back wifout resting, we could kill ourselves."

"I concur," I said with a nod.

"Me, too," Jane said.

We went back down the embankment, through the valley, up the other embankment, through the woods and to our old campsite. We were surprised to find the rest of the hikers already there. Thankfully, they had along a very large amount of meat.

It turned out that both Grant and Prof. Taylor's groups had found animals in the woods, and had managed to kill two wild pigs, three rabbits, and two deer. Apparently the plethora of game was due to the fact that they weren't being hunted in that neck of the woods.

"We must get this meat back to the passengers on the beach," Grant announced. "They've been waiting for food too long as it is."

"Before you decide on that," Colin cut in, "Jane, Rick and I also found somefing." He told them about the valley. "We also found the end of the island, about eight miles from here."

"Are you going to make a suggestion?" Grant asked. He sounded very tired, as did the rest of the group. I could picture us all collapsing from exhaustion before we reached the beach camp.

"I say we go back to the valley and rest for a few days. We've been goin' at a steady pace, and none of us are used to hiking this much. Except for maybe Zach and Karen, but I'm sure they'd like a rest."

I heard the aforementioned murmur consent.

"But the people at the beach need this food," Grant argued.

"And we need to rest. What good will it do them if we die before we get there?"

"Why don't we split up again?" suggested Paul peacefully. He usually stayed out of these arguments, but he was probably the most sensible person to decide things.

"Great," yawned Grant. "Who goes to the valley?" He paused to let them vote, apparently by a show of hands. "And who goes back to the beach? Okay, I'm the only one going to the beach. That's not going to work."

"How about using 'Bubble gum' again?" asked Zach.

Grant sighed deeply. "Okay."

As it turned out, Jane, Paul, and I got stuck going to the beach with Grant. I would have said I had bad luck, if I believed in luck.

"Rick, you don't have to go," Grant said. "We just need people to carry meat."

"Rick can carry it as well as I can," said Jane. "Can't you?" Was she actually *asking* me to go with them? That's what it sounded like.

"I, uh…" *Should I go swimming in a lush, green valley or hike for miles with the sun cooking me and probably whither away?* "Jane, can I talk to you?" We walked away from the group. "Do you want me to come and why?" I asked quietly.

She cleared her throat. "I don't agree with Grant all of the time. I don't really know this Paul guy; I don't know if he'll have my back in an argument. But you will."

Was she saying she needed me? "Fine, I'll go with you. But – I want one thing cleared up. I can't stand it anymore and I won't have a chance to ask you later. You don't really have a little brother, do you?"

"I have a sister," she said slowly.

"Stop using the 'You Look Like My Brother' technique on everybody. I don't know why you said it to Colin, but it's kind of obvious what you're doing."

"I don't know how else to make them back off," she said hoarsely.

"Nobody was really hitting on you, Jane. Why are you so sensitive? Is it because you feel guilty about your fiancé?"

"I told you not to mention that," she said sharply.

"No one can hear us," I retorted. "Stop being so edgy. You would be really nice if you'd just open up a little."

She didn't say anything. I realized I might have gone too far. "You sure you still want me to go with you?" I attempted at joking.

"Rick, if I did have a little brother, I'd want him to be like you." So apparently I was the perfect little brother for everyone.

"Why?" I asked bluntly.

"You see right through me. Sorry if that was worded wrong, but... I didn't used to be like this. But ever since the – since my –" She sighed. "I can't talk about it. But I didn't used to seem so walled up and fake. I was really good at acting, actually. I could convince people of anything. If you'd known me before, you wouldn't think I was the same person now."

"Jane, will you just try? Will you just try not to hide everything? You have nothing to hide, anyway."

"That's where you're wrong," she whispered. She led me back to the group, and I was once again left in a confused state as to who Jane Redford really was. It was seriously bugging me.

The group made a few rough sleds to carry the meat in. One sled for each deer and one sled for each of the pigs. The rabbits were just thrown on top. As we set up to leave, I heard the Professor talking to Grant. Some of the conversation was hard to catch. "...I still can't understand..." Grant said.

"...the animals, the plants...makes no sense at all. I keep thinking..."

"But why? How did they get here?"

I didn't understand the rest of it. I assumed there was something unusual about the animals they found.

We said our good-byes. Those that were staying said they would come back to the beach after a few days.

Grant, Paul, Jane and I dragged the animal-sleds across the fields. We made good time, and Grant said we'd gone about two miles when we made camp.

Day Thirteen, the next day, we continued our hike. It was particularly hot. I was glad I'd changed into cooler clothes after my 'bath,' and fortunately my skin had gotten used to sunlight and wasn't burning so bad. But between my back-pack, the sled, the heat, and lack of food, I could feel myself getting weak. At noon we stopped to take a break. I tried not to gulp down the water from my water-bottle.

"Dude," Paul huffed as he sat beside me. "This is so not fun."

I shoved the sleeves of my shirt higher onto my shoulders. "I need one of those little battery-powered travel fans."

Paul groaned. "Augh."

"You alright?"

"My stomach hurts," he said painfully.

"I need a hamburger really bad," I said wistfully. "And a strawberry shake, and blueberry pie, and a big steak-"

"Stop," he moaned, "stop. It's making me sick. I feel all queasy."

"You need to eat." I was getting a little worried about us. We hadn't eaten a full meal since we were in flight; if you can call airline food a solid meal.

"Yeah. We all look pretty bad. Poor Jane. All us guys are, like, soaked with sweat and she's a girl, you know. It's not cool for a girl to sweat. Grant looks like he's gonna faint any minute."

"Colin told him this was a stupid idea."

We continued with the stupid idea until late in the evening. About then, it started getting windy. We made camp and sat down to rest.

"This was a bad idea," Jane said tiredly. We all sounded like radios when the batteries are running out.

Grant snorted. "Yeah, it was. For us. Not for the people at the beach, though."

"Are we, like, at all close to the beach?" said Paul.

"We have about another day's walk."

Paul blew air through his teeth. "We are so gonna die."

"We won't die," said Grant.

"Yes we will. We've already gone through our extra water-bottles, and the ones we have now are half-full."

"Paul, we won't die," Jane assured him.

I thought Paul was being more dramatic than usual. I figured it was because the poor guy was sick. "Good-night," I said, and rolled onto my back. I fell asleep instantly.

Day Fourteen we woke up to high winds and glaring sunlight. We stumbled across the fields at an amazingly slow rate. I felt utterly exhausted. Even with the wind, I was sweating a lot, and I didn't have much water left in my bottle.

After a few hours, I heard Paul start groaning. I heard a thump, like he'd dropped onto the grass. "Paul?" I threw off my backpack and located him. I knelt beside him. "Paul, answer me."

"I can't do it," he rasped. "Sorry, dudes, I gotta rest."

I touched his arm. It felt clammy.

"Paul, what happened?" asked Jane as she knelt next to me.

"I got all dizzy," he said in a shaky voice. "I got all c-c-cold all of a sudden…"

"Is he okay?" I choked. I was scared. So many bad things had happened already. "Is he okay?!" I shouted when no one answered me.

"He's suffering from heat exhaustion," said Jane. "Grant, do you have any extra shirts? We need them to wrap around Paul."

"I'll see what I can do," Grant answered. I heard him stumble over to his bag.

"We have to get water," Jane sighed. "Rick, have you got any left?"

"Hardly."

"He's going to dehydrate." She was using the same voice as she did when Colin was hurt: strong but sympathetic. "We need to get him water now."

"How are we going to do that?" Grant was back. He was breathing heavily. I suddenly noticed Jane and I were, too.

"What if we all have heat exhaustion?" I asked. "How are we going to get water?"

"How far away are we from the caves?" Jane asked Grant.

"About two and a half miles."

"I can go," she said with confidence. I heard her opening the backpacks. "I'll take the extra water bottles and go to the spring. You two stay here. Keep him wrapped up, and keep giving him water. Try to keep the sun directly off his face."

Thunder rumbled, and the wind picked up.

"It's going to rain. That's just great," said Grant bitterly.

"Actually, it is great," Jane said as she zipped up her pack. "You can collect the rain water in your bottles. I'll hurry."

"Jane," Grant said, stopping her. "You can't make it there and back. Let me go."

"No. You're more exhausted than I am, I can see that."

"That could change quickly if you hike for two miles back and forth."

"I'm more used to these sorts of situations than you are," she said firmly.

I turned my head in her direction. "What does that mean?"

She didn't answer me. "Grant, please, just stay here. I'll be back."

It was a pretty awful wait. Paul started complaining of muscle cramps. I figured that was probably bad. He started breathing rapidly.

Grant didn't sound too good, either. I didn't feel peachy, but I was too scared about the other three to be sick. I leaned over Paul's face to keep the sun off. I started praying. *Don't let us die, God. Keep Jane from passing out. If anything, let it rain like crazy, God. We really need water, and the clouds will take care of the sun. Come on, after all the stuff you've had me go through I at least deserve rain!*

I felt the heat of the sun lessening, until it was gone completely. "How cloudy is it?" I asked Grant.

"Uhhh…" He sounded awful. "It looks like a storm." After a while he said, "I shouldn't have let her go by herself."

"She'll make it. It's a straight walk across the fields."

As time went on, I was beginning to doubt my statement. Especially once it started to rain. Fortunately it wasn't a strong rain, although the wind was pretty sharp. Now I was cold; I dug in my backpack and found the sweater Grant gave me. I remembered Jane said we should wrap stuff around Paul. I was freezing, but I didn't want my friend to suffer, either.

"You should wear it," Grant said. He must have seen my hesitation. "He's fine. And your skin is turning blue."

"Great. Now we can die of hypothermia." I pulled the sweater over my head and wrapped my arms around my body. This was very bad. First we sweat and then we freeze.

I refused to get sick. I hated being sick. I heard thunder booming in the distance. "Are we on high ground?"

"Yeah."

"So…will we be hit by lightening?"

He muttered something unintelligible. I assumed that was a "Probably."

It was pretty scary to be in such a bad situation and not be able to see what was going on. I could only feel cold, hear the storm, smell the rain, and taste it dripping into my mouth.

"Are you okay, Rick?" Grant moved closer to me. "You look really scared." Grant was really nice, sometimes, and usually at the weirdest times. It kept throwing me for a loop.

"Yeah, I'm scared. It's like being in a nightmare that you can't wake up from, and you never know what's out there in the dark until it gets you."

"Have you been having nightmares?"

"Actually, I haven't dreamed since we crashed, thank God. If I did they'd be bad."

"I keep dreaming I'm running after someone, but I never see who it is. I keep thinking it was the CIA agent that messed things up in England." He was slowly slipping back into Logical Grant.

"Why are you chasing him?"

"It's a long story," he said, and I thought he shivered. "Basically it was a top-level undercover agent that was planted with their partner in England to integrate themselves into an underground terrorist community to spy on them. That cell was funding numerous other terrorist cells, as well as funding weapons of mass destruction."

"Whoa. In England?"

"There are bad guys everywhere you go. Anyway, something happened and one of the two agents was killed. The other agent took revenge and blew up a bank which the terrorists were using as a front. The British got mad because they were trying to gather information from the terrorists to ascertain when their next big attack was. Anyway, the agent disappeared, and only a few people really know who it was, anyway, because the agent was undercover. But I had to go settle down the Brits." His voice was winding down towards the end. I thought at first he was feeling better but obviously he was still exhausted.

"Were there any civilians in the bank when it blew up?"

"No. I don't think there were any people in there at all at the time. The agent destroyed their HQ, though. Set them back a lot." I heard his voice shake like he shivered.

"So the agent did a good thing?"

"Well…they didn't exactly do a bad thing, but it was against orders. They're in major trouble for messing up a lot of procedures that were set in place. They should have just gone to a safe-house. Revenge is never the right answer."

He didn't talk again for a long time. I wondered whether he'd passed out. "Grant?"

He didn't answer.

"Paul?"

"Yeah, man?" he said weakly. His breathing was still too fast.

"Just wanted to make sure you're okay. Where's Grant?"

"Think he's on look-out for Jane. He was collecting rain water."

"Oh, geez, I completely forgot about that."

"Grant didn't."

"Paul…do you think he's weird?"

"Nah. He's dedicated."

"Are we really going to die?" I was surprised I'd asked.

"Nah," he said again.

Thunder rumbled, and the rain started falling harder. I tucked my knees under my chin. "I'm scared."

"Yeah. I heard you tell Grant. It's okay, you can be scared. You're just a kid."

I had forgotten I was a kid. It made me more scared but less embarrassed for being so.

Grant came back and handed me a water bottle. "Drink it all, slowly," he said. "They take forever to fill up."

I drank about half the bottle. "Here, Paul, you take the rest."

"No, man," he breathed. "You drink it. I'm okay, really." I heard him move. "Augh, man, I'm dizzy."

I heard Grant start to stand up. He breathed in sharply. "Me, too. Rick?"

"I dunno if I'm dizzy," I answered. "I know I'm really, really wet."

"I am such a jerk," said Grant, "letting Jane go like that. It's been a long time now."

I wasn't able to keep track of time very well, but I was worrying about her, too.

"She was in better shape than you were, dude," Paul reassured him. "Besides, she didn't walk there in the sun very much."

"*Why* was she in better shape than me?" Grant thought aloud.

"Don't be jealous, dude," Paul said.

Grant sighed. "I hope she's okay…" He paused. "Is that…? Oh, my G-" He never actually finished the sentence, and I thought for sure he'd fallen over dead.

"What…happened?" I asked slowly.

"Jane!" Grant shouted.

"Jane's back?" I said in a way that sounded like a three-year-old saying "Mommy's back?"

"Anybody thirsty?" she said as she walked up, breathless.

"Are you okay?" Grant said, and he probably started to stand up.

"Whoa," Jane said. It was confusing, but I think Grant had another dizzy spell and Jane sat him down.

"Is everybody alright?" she panted.

"We're not dead," Paul rasped.

"Here," said Jane, and I heard Paul gulping water. "Rick?" she asked, "You okay?"

I had a sudden urge to hug her and never let go. Only because it would be too embarrassing to hug Grant, and Paul seemed too fragile. While I was thinking that out logically, I figured that, logically, it would be too juvenile to hug her. Never mind that I was a juvenile. But, I still thought better of hugging her.

"Fine," I said flatly.

"Oh, that hike was awful," Jane groaned. "But worth it," she added quickly.

Grant laughed quietly. "I'm sorry I let you do it."

"Don't be ridiculous, Grant," she sighed. "You couldn't have done it."

They mumbled a small argument. I scooted closer to Paul. "Do you feel better?"

"Sure," he said good-naturedly. "Sorry for freaking out before. When we wake up tomorrow we'll all feel better."

I let out a sigh of relief. "If you're okay, and Grant's okay enough to argue again, it's my turn to be sick." So saying, I laid down in the wet grass and fell asleep.

Chapter 12

"Rick," she called gently.

"Not now, Mom," I answered, my voice thick.

"Rick," she said, laughing a little.

Oh, great. Biggest mistake ever. I'd just forgotten who and where I was and called Jane 'Mom.'

I opened my eyes, forgetting, also, that I didn't have to open my eyes. I brushed my hands through my hair. "What?"

"Time to go."

I groaned loudly. *Are we ever going to stop hiking? Are we ever going to get off this stupid island?!* I was in a mood that some people would call 'waking up on the wrong side of the bed,' except I hadn't slept in a bed, and frankly I didn't see why a certain side mattered.

"How are you feeling?" Jane said in very kind way. I wished I could see her face.

"Fine," I said, very untruthfully. I had a feeling this was going to be the kind of day when the exhaustion and pain of the last two weeks caught up with me. I stood up unsteadily and pulled the sweater off. "So you guys are all healthy now?"

"You were sick, too."

I made a face. "No."

She paused. "We're okay enough to drag the sleds to the beach camp."

"Then, when we get there, we'll probably sleep for a few days," Paul said, and I could hear a smile in his voice. I thanked God he was okay.

We hiked across the slightly soggy fields, all of us still damp from the day before. It wasn't sunny enough to dry us out, and we all felt sticky because of the humid weather.

"It'll rain again today," said Grant.

"Well, I'm getting used to being soggy," I said.

"Paul, you still okay?" asked Jane breathlessly.

Paul grunted. "I'll tell you if I have to stop."

"Dear God, I'm sick of hiking," Jane said through her teeth.

Grant launched another speech. "But if we didn't do this, the people at the-"

Jane cut him off. "Grant! Now is not the time." They started arguing, but I didn't care what it was about.

I heard the wind rustling the grass, and a bird call, far off. I was sure that if we'd come here on a tropical island cruise, this place would be beautiful. In fact, I'd always wanted to go on a cruise. Somehow I didn't think that this particular time spent on the island counted as R&R.

We got to the camp by late afternoon. As we approached, we could hear a disturbance, like the people were fighting amongst themselves.

I heard Grant sigh. "Here we go again."

As we got closer, Grant said "Stop." There was a pause, like he was watching for something. His voice dropped to a harsh whisper. "Leave the sleds near these trees. We'll back-track and get behind those rock formations on the beach."

Paul and Jane seemed to understand why we were behaving like this. Jane took my arm and I followed them. I waited to talk until we were behind one of the rocks. "Anybody want to fill the blind guy in?" I whispered.

"There's something weird going on at the beach," Grant answered. "We're about a half a mile away from them, so it's hard to tell, but it looks like they're all standing in a circle and someone is guarding them. Jane, did we bring a pair of binoculars?"

"There were two pairs," she sighed, "Colin has one and Prof. Taylor has one."

He took a moment to think. "Okay, Jane and Paul, you come with me. We'll stay behind the tree-line and get closer."

"What do you think is going on?" asked Jane.

Grant clicked his tongue. "I think it's the natives. I think they've captured the other passengers."

"Why would they do that?" asked Paul. "Are they going to kill- um, I mean, what are they gonna do with 'em, like, ransom 'em?" I supposed he'd cut himself off because I was sitting there.

Thunder rumbled. Tiny drops of rain started hitting me in the face.

"Let's go," Grant said. "Rick, do not move." They crunched off through the sand.

I was all alone.

The surf was pounding angrily against the beach, and I hoped I was far enough away from the sea that it wouldn't reach me. I pulled my knees up to my chin and waited for my friends to come back. I felt very alone, very tired. I felt so insignificant, so small and helpless in the big, black ocean of the world.

This wasn't good. I hated feeling like this. I remembered all the promises I'd made, not to be bitter, not to hate the world, that I was lucky I was alive. So far I hadn't acted on any of that. I wanted to sit here until I could accept everything: mom and dad's death, Noah's death, my terrible predicament on this island; most of all, being blind.

I had a small urge to pray, that that would at least let me know someone cared that I was down here on this awful island, but I kept pushing the idea aside, I didn't know why.

Suddenly I heard shouts. It sounded like the passengers were rioting against the natives. I heard a gun shot, and hoped no one would be killed. People were really yelling now, and there were more gun shots. It sounded like they were going for an all-out war. Then I heard – and at first I didn't believe it – a horse, a real horse, give a frightening whinnying sound.

I tucked my head between my knees and covered my ears. This was too bizarre; this was too crazy and sad for me to take anymore. I didn't know how long I stayed balled up, my heart throbbing in my ears. Then a hand touched my head. My eyes flew open and I lifted my head, expecting to hear Jane tell me we'd better run for it.

"Don't move," a British voice said, but I didn't recognize it. It was a woman's voice. "What are you doing here?"

"Trying not to be killed," I said hoarsely.

"Stand up," the voice commanded.

I could still hear shouts on the beach. I stood up stiffly. "Who are you?"

"That's not for you to know." It wasn't a purely British accent, now that I thought about it...I didn't know what it was.

"What the heck are you talking about? Why aren't you over there fighting the natives with the rest-"

"Why aren't you fighting the natives, young man?"

"I can't." I swallowed. I felt a rush of air in front of my face. "What are you doing?"

"You can't see," the person said slowly.

I imagined she'd waved her hand in front of my face. "You haven't heard about me yet?"

Obviously she hadn't. "What are these packs for?"

"You don't seem too fazed by the fact that there's a small revolution going on behind us."

"My people will have them in order shortly."

"Oh, my God." It hit me like a brick. She was one of them. She was a native. There was only one thing I could do to get away from her, and that was to run. I could tell where she was standing, right there in front of me. As she started to talk again, I went into a line-backer position and rammed her full in the chest, knocking her down. I tripped over her and ran like mad across the sand. I had no idea where I was going. The rain pelted me in the face. I tried to stay in a straight line by listening to the surf. I heard the native woman shout something.

As I picked up my speed, I thought I was home-free. Until I felt a giant weight come crashing down on my back. I hit the sand hard.

"Don't move!" Another native voice, this time a man's. He was tying up my hands while sitting on my back, and since I could barely breathe, I figured it was best to comply. He dragged me to my feet and led me back to the rocks.

The native lady put her hand on my chest. "Your heart is beating very fast. Are you scared?"

"Duh," I panted.

"Where did you learn to do that?"

"What, run? Where I come from, you learn that at an early age." I couldn't believe I was being sarcastic to a native. Then again, politeness wouldn't help me if they were planning to kill me, anyway.

"But you're blind. Your courage to escape was fascinating."

"Yeah, well, I kind of enjoy being alive."

She actually laughed. "I won't kill you."

"Who are you, anyway?" I said, cutting to the chase. "Where'd you come from?"

"We'll talk later."

"Figures."

The big native guy hauled me across the beach, right to where the passengers' camp was. The noise of fighting had stopped. I could tell we were standing under the trees. I heard the leaves rustling above my head.

"As long as you people remain on this side of the mountain range, we shall not harass you any longer," boomed a deep voice, another native.

"That's a deal," I heard Grant say. I was surprised at how glad I was he'd made it. It sounded like the chief of the natives and our leader (Grant) were making a peace treaty.

"And this pact will remain so for a year's time," Chief continued, "beginning in thirteen days."

"What happens after a year?" Grant asked.

"At that time, all will fall into place."

"What does that mean?" It was hard not to answer Grant when he used that tone.

"By then, only the best of you people will have survived. Ask no more."

"Take him now, we are leaving," the native lady whispered.

At that moment the man holding me clamped his hand over my mouth and began dragging me away from the beach. I kicked and writhed my way out of his grasp. "HELP!" I screamed. Then I felt something heavy hit me in the head, and I blacked out.

I really disliked blacking out, as it had happened too many times to appreciate. I awoke with my hands and legs tied together.

"So you are awake," said the native lady.

"I suppose you've taken me far enough away that no one can hear me scream."

I heard her chuckle. "Do you know why I've taken you?" That sounded rhetorical. "You are a novelty. We owe respect to people with a gift of wit and courage such as you have, especially if that person is already inhibited by a handicap."

"So give me a Nobel Prize and let me go back to the beach."

"You have such an amusing way of talking." Her voice was echoing slightly.

"Are we in a cave?"

She laughed again. I didn't know what this woman found so funny, but it was slightly unnerving. She obviously didn't care if I was ready to knock her down again to get away. "We're in the cave by the water supply. I think you know where that is."

"How do you know I know?"

"I heard quite a few of you have been here. And, you must have found the spring to survive."

"You 'heard'…so, you guys have been watching us?"

"Somewhat."

Being in the cave reminded me of what happened to Colin and the hunting party. I wasn't about to mention I thought her people were low life murderers, but the anger must have shown on my face.

"The hunting party that we ambushed…they were on our hunting grounds. They had no right to be there."

"You had no right to kill them," I said quietly.

"You don't know our ways."

"Yeah? What are your ways? Who are you?"

She took her time preparing to tell me. "In 1789, England sent a ship of convicts to start an exploratory settlement in a new land."

Judging from what she said, she was probably talking about what would now be Australia. At around the date she mentioned, they were shipping convicts over there to colonize it.

"They were what people called religious fanatics, insane, thieves and murderers." Her voice was strangely sympathetic.

"They sailed across the vast oceans for many days, south to where the storms were terrible, and then northeast towards their final destination. In that time on the ship, the convicts became united. They were all searching for the answer to life, and found the answer together."

"What's the answer?" I asked when she paused.

"Natural Existence. We're supposed to live in harmony with nature."

"So...no modern conveniences?"

"Oh, yes, of course. We have created a new source of power to generate the machines we use. But we never forget our roots. Everything, eventually, comes down to the basics of nature, which we incorporate into everything."

"What happened to the convicts?"

"The ship met a terrible storm-"

"And was blown off course?" *All too familiar.*

"Yes. Far, far past the land they would have settled in. When the ship crashed on this island, the convicts overtook their captors and began their own colony here, putting into practice their new religion. Those who wouldn't join in were killed. Death is simply an inevitable part of nature, after all. They were our ancestors. We have continued in their beliefs, serving the island."

"You, uh, worship the island?"

"Yes. It gives us all we need. Food, water-"

"What about the plants you brought from England?"

"Oh, you know about them. Yes, the convicts had seed for planting when they reached the new land, as well as live-stock. It is all the same basics of nature."

"So...you worship the island, which gives you every-thing. What about rain to grow things?"

"I said we worshipped natural living."

"But you have machines. Is that natural?"

"As long as we have the basics-"

"Why did you kill the hunting group? Was that natural?"

"You people don't believe in what we believe. You are dangerous to nature. You need to die."

I swallowed audibly. *I'll just keep my mouth shut before she murders me in the name of Nature.*

"Those men were going to kill the animals that the island meant for us to have. It was wrong. So we killed them."

I just nodded.

"It may take you a while to come to understand our ways. What is your name, young man?"

I considered lying, but it wouldn't do me any good. "Rick. Uh, that's short for Richard."

"Richard is a fine, noble name. I am Helen. I am the wife of our leader, Theodoric. We're taking you to our settlement. You may stay with us, and become one of us."

I was about to tell her not a snowball's chance I was living with such crazy people, but decided it might be wiser to play along. "How long will I be, uh, with you?"

"When you are one of us, you are one of us forever. If you decide not to become a part of our religion, we shall still reward you with the hero's ceremony, because of your adversity over the hardships that have befallen you. It is our duty to honor you."

"Hero's ceremony...for death, I guess? So I go out in style?"

She laughed again. "There is no need for worry. You will come to our ways."

I nodded again. "What's going to happen to all the airplane survivors after a year?"

"We have talked enough," she said softly. "All will be revealed in that time."

I heard her walk away. It sounded like the natives were standing outside the cave, talking. I tried getting my hands out of the ropes. It rubbed skin off my wrists, but I had loosened it. I got to my knees and twisted to untie the ropes on my ankles. It worked. My hands were still tied together. After a lot of painful maneuvers I got my hands underneath my behind and then I slipped my legs through. I used my teeth to help untie my hands.

I listened. It sounded like they were heading towards the spring. Unfortunately, I had no idea if someone was standing guard over me. I got back down on the ground and pretended I was choking to death. Nobody came to my rescue. I got back up and felt my way along the cave wall to the entrance.

That's when I stopped. *How the heck do you think you're getting back to the beach?* I asked myself. I didn't have my walking stick, and I wasn't sure what direction led to the beach. I also had no idea, if I ran, whether the natives would see me. It was like knowing there were snipers hidden in the hills and I was walking right through the middle of the valley.

This is not the time for analogies, Rick. When I was in the cave, after Colin was shot, Grant mentioned that the ravine behind the cave went all the way down to the beach. If I could get to the ravine now, I could follow it. Like it's that simple. I didn't know why I wasn't waiting until I was sure the natives couldn't see me, like at night. There was just something really scary about them. Like when she mentioned my hero ceremony for death.

I breathed deeply a few times. Then I dashed to the outside of the cave. Running my hand along the rock wall, I ran. When the wall rounded off to the side, I knew I was at the back of the cave. There were some trees I had to get through, then I'd be at the ravine.

"What are you doing?" a voice called quietly behind me. It was a girl's voice, probably a teenager's. It was native. I was caught.

Chapter 13

"Darn it," I muttered lamely. This was highly upsetting. Now they'd kill me for sure, hero ceremony or no. I turned around and held up my hands. "Got me."

"You are not planning to become one of us, then?"

"Duh." These people had a habit of stating the obvious. "Are you going to cuff me?"

"Uh...I'm not sure what that means. I'm not taking you back, if that's what you mean."

My jaw dropped. "You – you're not going to tell them I'm running away?"

She paused. "I believe that if I honor you with a favor, I shall be smiled upon by Fate."

"That's...cool. Who are you?"

"I am Chloe. I'm Theodoric and Helen's daughter. You're Rick. I heard you talking to my mother."

"Cool. Okay, so I'll go now."

"Wait." I heard her rush over to me. She stood very close to me.

"What...are you doing?" I asked uncomfortably.

"You really can't see, can you?" I didn't answer her. "I'm sorry you won't become one of us. You will die, you know," she added softly.

"Uh, yeah, I'm going now."

She grabbed my hand. "Get out of here," she whispered. "All of you; get off the island before the year is up."

"Why?"

"You will die."

"How?"

"They'll kill you."

"Why are you telling me this?"

"Because I don't believe you are meant to die. But the others won't see that."

I sighed. "Believe me, I'll do my best to get out of here. Look, uh, thank you for helping me. I hope Fate, um, smiles…or whatever on…you…bye."

"Good-bye," Chloe said, kissing my hand respectfully. "May we both be blessed. I'll try to detain the others." I heard her rush off.

I wiped my hand on my pants and wound my way through the trees. At the edge of the ravine, I sat down. "Here we go again." I pushed off and slid to the bottom, where I had a nasty meeting with a bunch of sharp rocks. It was nothing serious, but my knees would be sore for a while. It wasn't a very deep ravine, and it wasn't wide. Its bottom was extremely uneven, which was not accommodating to someone with balance issues. I tripped over roots and rocks every three feet. I was half-running, which didn't help, but I wasn't about to slow down, and I couldn't hold my arms out to keep my balance because it was so narrow.

It began raining a lot harder on me, which was less than helpful with my attitude. There were already big puddles covering the ravine bottom, but as the rain came down in sheets, I was standing in a small river. I knew immediately that this could turn into a dangerous situation. I heard a roaring sound coming from behind me. I only had a second to go into a panic, and then I started climbing up the ravine's wall. I wouldn't make it up the cliffs, so I was heading up to regular ground-level.

The problem was that the rain made the ravine edge slippery. My heart was pounding, practically vibrating my ribcage. I couldn't get a good hand hold on any rocky surfaces. I could hear the swell of water coming towards me.

I still couldn't find any hand holds. Rain beat me in the face. My heart thumped.

"I am not going to die on this stupid island!" I shouted in anger, to nothing - and to everything - in particular. I dug my fingers into some mud and hauled myself up. I clawed at the surface above the ravine and hoisted myself up onto the ground. As I rolled onto the grass I heard a wave of water rush through the ravine below me. Breathing hard, I stood up and stumbled forward, feeling a tree in front of me. I leaned on it and caught my breath. At that moment, I heard a voice. It sounded like it was calling my name. I rushed forward, going around trees, then stopped. I didn't hear it again.

Great, now I'm going nuts. I wasn't about to call out, just in case the voice was real and it was the natives coming to get me and drag me back to kill me (honorably).

"Rick!" Whoever it was, they were going to find me. I didn't know where to run. "Rick!" The person was closer. I wished I'd died in the ravine. It would have been much better than being murdered ceremoniously. "Rick!" They could see me now, I was sure. They sounded relieved they'd finally found me.

Suddenly, I really, really, didn't want to die, not in so awful a way. Not that I could save myself. I couldn't see which way to get out of there. I was a sitting duck, and a blind one at that.

As the person got closer, I froze. I had a panic attack. I couldn't get out of there. I screamed, since it was the only defense mechanism I had.

"Rick!" The person tried to grab my arms and I decked them. I kicked at them. I wasn't going to die that easily.

All of a sudden they flipped me onto my back and pinned my arms behind me, knocking the air out of my lungs. "Rick, for Pete's sake, it's me, Jane."

"How was I supposed to know that?!" I shouted.

She let my arms go and pulled me to my feet. "Are you okay?"

I wished I could glare at her. *"Do I look okay to you?"*

"Man, Rick, cool it," Jane said sarcastically. "I came out here to rescue you. We've had a search party going since the natives took you yesterday. I heard you yell a minute ago, and headed in this direction. Maybe I should have left you alone," she added.

"You didn't have to rescue me," I said bitterly, water pouring off my nose. "I was escaping on my own."

"You couldn't have made it to the beach." She wasn't mean. She was sympathetic, which I translated into pity, which set me off.

"I could have made it!"

"You'd have died first," she said reasonably. "If the natives wanted to take you, then they're looking for you now. They'd find you."

"I'd make it." I spat rainwater from my mouth.

"Don't be stubborn."

"I'm not stubborn! Everybody pities me, there's nothing wrong with me!"

"You are blind, Rick!" It was a fact, but it was so blunt and so true that it hurt immensely to hear it. Jane touched my shoulder. "What happened to you? First you were accepting everything that happened, and now you're going absolutely crazy."

"I have to go crazy!" I shouted. "I have to go absolutely insane! I've never gone crazy in my entire life, even when I had a good reason! I've always contained it, always been strong, and it's awful! For one day, just one, I need to yell at somebody! Everybody! Today seemed like a pretty good candidate! Just about every bad thing that could happen to somebody happened to me! Why me? I'm fourteen years old, Jane. I'm a kid. I don't deserve any of this." I caught my breath. "You know what I want?" I had pretty much stopped yelling. "I want five minutes, just five, to be able to see again. I want to see my family. I want to tell them good-bye."

"Rick...I understand-"

"No, you don't," I said, winding down.

"Yes, I do," she said sharply.

"How?" She didn't answer. "How, Jane? And don't say you can't tell me."

"What do you want from me?" she asked emotionally.

"I want to know who you are! I want you to tell me, right now, who you are."

"I can't tell you."

"Oh, stop hiding! I know you aren't really an insurance saleswoman."

"Yes, I am!" she argued.

"Yeah? Then explain to me what that move was you used to flipped me onto the ground a minute ago? C'mon, Jane. You keep telling all these stories to hide yourself. You didn't really ever have a fiancé, did you? And he didn't die."

"Yes, he did!" she yelled.

"Stop it, Jane!"

"He died! I watched Eric die!" She was crying.

I nodded. "How'd he die, Jane?"

She tried to hold back her tears. "That rogue agent that Grant had to go apologize for in England...that was me."

I felt my mouth fall open. I should have seen it. The easy personality switches, the cover-ups, the survival skills...the kickboxing. Duh, Rick. "Grant kind of told me the story."

"Did he tell you how they killed my fiancé, Rick? Someone told them who we were. They caught us and tortured Eric for information, and made me sit there and watch. Then they shot him in the chest and held me in the chair so I could watch him bleed to death."

"Did you get to say good-bye?"

She breathed in shakily. "I tried. I hoped he heard me. I couldn't watch him any more. I fought off the guards, grabbed one of their guns, shot them. I wanted to save Eric." She started crying again. "I couldn't. All I could do was tell him I loved him. I kissed him and he died. He just died. There was nothing I could do." She broke down into sobs.

I wasn't sure what to say. I walked slowly towards her and wrapped my arms around her. Nobody hugged me when my family died, but I realized I had wanted that. I had wanted somebody to be there for me. I guess that in the end I wanted not necessarily pity, but sympathy.

"They killed him, Rick, right there in front of me. They killed the person I loved the most. So I destroyed their life-time of work. I wasn't going to kill anyone, but I wanted to hurt them, badly."

"Did it help to blow up their building?"

"Yeah. I found it ironic that I could save the world, but I couldn't save one man." She was still crying, and I wasn't going to stop her. "I fell apart. There was a giant hole in my heart, and I couldn't tell anyone how much it hurt."

"Why were you going back to LA?"

"I figured it was time to face up to the facts. I went against procedures and acted on revenge. I don't care what they do to me. I just want to go home."

"So do I."

She put her arms around me and cried into my shoulder. I let her cry for a long time. After all, she had let me go crazy for a few moments. Now we both felt better. I would probably be able to keep all of those promises I'd made to myself, and she'd get over her fiancé dying. Maybe she'd even stop using the 'You're Like My Little Brother' Technique.

Hey, God? Sorry about all that crazy stuff. I should have talked to you in the first place. I guess you know what's going on. I really hate the way things are going down, but you've granted me miraculous life this long…you must have a plan of some kind.

Jane pulled away eventually. "Great time to be stuck without Kleenex, huh?" she sniffed.

I smiled.

"I'm sorry, Rick, that you had to go through all this terrible stuff."

"Me too, for you. Hey, what's your real name?"

"Actually it is Jane. Jane Cutter."

"Still sounds like an actress," I laughed.

"On the flight I was using an alias that the CIA had given me. Which is why, when Grant wanted to find the manifest, I took it and destroyed it. If he saw the alias name, he might get suspicious. That 9mm was mine too, and that would've given me away for sure."

"Do you think the CIA or whatever is going to arrest you?"

She sighed. "I don't want them to catch me, I want to turn myself in. It'll look better. I'm a top agent. I've gotten in and out of trouble before. I can probably do it again."

"Good."

"Sorry for crying on you."

I shrugged. "It's not like I could get any wetter."

She laughed, her genuine laugh. I figured she'd sound genuine from now on.

Chapter 14

As we walked back, I asked Jane what had happened at the beach.

"Apparently the natives came and ambushed them. They were questioning them to see where the rest of us were. Then Grant shot one of the guards, and one of the people from the beach had the gun we left behind, so he started shooting, and then the natives started shooting at us with arrows, and people were fighting them and escaping and a horse almost trampled somebody. Then the native leader called a halt and started talking things out with Grant."

"Did anybody die?"

"Five passengers, and a native, and a few people were injured."

"Are the dead people...anybody you and I know especially?"

"No."

When we got to the beach, it stopped raining. A bunch of people came to tell me how glad they were that I was okay. Paul came up and grabbed me in a bear hug. "Dude, we were really worried."

I hugged him back. Grant came up and started demanding to know things. "Where did they take you? Who are they? Are the natives planning to attack again?"

"First off," I said tiredly, "they aren't natives. They're Naturalists."

"'Naturalists?'" Grant repeated.

"Well...basically, that's what they are." I related what Helen told me, leaving out the hero ceremony thing. "Second, I don't believe they'll bother us for a year."

"How'd you get away?" someone asked.

"I untied myself and ran. I followed the ravine, and then Jane found me."

After my small press conference, Paul said I should rest. We went to the tree-line and sat down. "They've decided to build a raft, you know," Paul said.

"No, I didn't know. Out of what?"

"Trees and pieces of the plane. It's gonna take forever to build, and nobody's sure how to build it, but as soon as that Chief dude said we only had a year, they started comin' up with ways to get out of here. They'll sail as far as they can 'til they find a passing ship."

"Who's going to go on the raft? I mean, we won't all fit, will we?"

"They haven't decided that yet. Although I have this feeling Grant is going."

"Huh. This'll be interesting. My dad was a carpenter, you know."

"Really? Then you can help us out. Are you any good at it?"

I smiled. "Well, I won first place at the Junior Carver's Competition. I beat a nineteen-year-old." I shook my head. "I don't think I could do that now, though."

"You can always relearn it. If anybody can, you can."

"I guess it's possible." I leaned against a tree and rubbed my stomach. "I've probably lost about ten pounds already. I am so hungry."

"Oh, dude, sorry! We got food! You know that stuff we dragged over here? We're like, trying to preserve some of it, and the rest we cooked up last night. Had a regular feast. I'll get you some."

"I would be eternally grateful."

I had experienced the taste of venison once when in France with Noah. Though that deer was outlandishly expensive and prepared by gourmet chefs, the one I ate now tasted a hundred times better. Paul laughed at how I gulped it down. I was a little queasy afterward, but I felt like I'd eaten an entire meal. I guzzled a bottle of water as Paul laughed at me. "Feel better?"

"Much," I sighed. "Not just the food. I feel better about everything."

"Really?" he asked curiously. "A near death experience helped, huh?"

"Do you mean the natives capturing me or almost choking on the venison?" I laughed. "I don't know. I'm just okay now."

"Those natives are freaky."

"Technically they aren't natives. They came from – what are you laughing at?" I asked when he snorted.

"Just you. You're so…analytical."

"Please." I shook my head. "How does Jane look?"

He paused. "Why? You think she's hot or-"

"No! Yuck! Don't be weird, man. I just want to know if she looks happy."

"She looks happy. She looks pretty. Beautiful, actually. She looks better. What'd you say to her? She left the woods practically crying that you were dead, an' all grim, she comes back lookin' like that."

"What can I say?" I said with a coy smile, "Girls like analytical short guys."

"With sunburn."

"I have sunburn?"

"Hmmm…do you?"

"That's not funny," I said, pushing him. "Have you ever been kissed by an admirer?"

"What? Jane kissed you?!"

"Ssshhh!" I clamped my hands over his face, covering his mouth. "Absolutely not! That would be sick! Who said we were talking about Jane, you doofus? I meant a native girl."

"*What?*" he said, his voice muffled.

"Yeah. I'm a hero as far as they're concerned."

"No way."

"They were going to give me a ceremony," I said importantly.

"No way," he repeated.

"Her name was Chloe," I went on, taking my hands off of his mouth and drinking more water.

"What are you guys whispering about?" whined a familiar voice. I inhaled the scent of coconut tanning lotion.

"Sup, Dana?" Paul said. "Rick got kissed by a native girl."

"Paul!" I said incredulously, half choking. I was just about to tell him I was kidding.

"Oh." She sounded shocked. "Well, uh, I was supposed to tell you that that Grant guy wants to talk to Rick. He really got kissed?"

"No," I said, shaking my head emphatically. "No, no, no, I was kidding. She didn't - not like you think. It was - she was –"

"He's a hero, you know," went on Paul. "The native folks were going to give him a big ceremony."

"What'd you run away for?" Dana asked sourly. "Sounds like you were having fun." I heard her walk away.

"Paul!" I said, disbelievingly. "What did you do that for?"

"I just wanted to see what she'd say. She's such a Drama Queen."

"Grant's gonna quiz me if he hears about it, and I'm telling him you made it up."

"I didn't."

"She kissed my hand, okay? Like a blessing. She believes Fate will...smile on her or something, I don't know. She was missing some marbles. She let me get away."

"She must think you're cute. Except for the sunburn."

"I don't have sunburn."

"Yes, you do. I'm not kidding, man. Your forehead is peeling."

"What?" I reached up to touch my head. "Ow." I peeled what felt like skin off.

"That's not skin, that's tree-sap," he said, leaning close to me.

"You let me walk around with tree-sap on my head? Some friend you are."

"How'd it get there?"

"When I came out of the ravine I leaned on a tree. What'll I do?"

"Jump in the ocean and rub it off."

I considered. "Fine." Paul and I went to the ocean and I jumped in. I was used to being wet now. I scrubbed at my head.

"Rick!" I heard Grant call. "Rick, did Dana tell you I wanted to talk to you?"

"Oh yeah," I said, my head half submerged. "I was just washing off this-" a wave rippled over my face.

"I needed to ask you some questions."

"-sap," I finished.

There was a small pause. "Excuse me?" Grant asked sharply.

"Not you. I mean, you're not a sap, I've got sap on my – forget it. What do you want?" I shook my head to get the water off my face. "Is it off, Paul?"

"Yeah."

Grant cleared his throat. "I'd like to know what happened from the beginning. I need to know what kind of people we're dealing with."

"Sure. Where's my luggage?" I asked, coming out of the water and pulling off my shirt.

"Wow," said Paul, "you did lose a few pounds."

"Thanks."

"Can we talk?" asked poor Grant, exasperated.

We found my luggage and I changed into a new shirt and pants, then we sat down to talk. It was made obvious we were keeping this meeting low key and between a few people (Grant, Jane, Paul, me, and a couple guys who were sort of new recruits, Jim and Kirk).

I told them how I ran when Helen found me, and how they'd recaptured me and taken me to the caves. I told them what she'd said about their ancestors. "She gave a reason for killing the hunting party."

"Which was?"

"They were hunting the animals the island meant for the Naturalists to have. She says we don't understand them, we threaten nature or something, and we need to die."

"She said we need to die?" Grant clarified.

"M-hm." I nodded slowly. "She wouldn't say what they'll do to us after a year, but I have a feeling it's bad."

"'Only the best of you will have survived,'" quoted Jim (or Kirk) thoughtfully.

"Listen, they told me I was a hero," I told them. "For... my adversity over hardship. If I didn't join their tribe, they were going to give me a hero's ceremony before they killed me. Maybe that's what they're planning on doing to 'the best of us.'"

They were quiet for a while.

"Also," I went on, giving more grim news, "after I untied myself and got near the ravine, one of the natives found me.

She was the Chief's daughter, but she said she'd let me go so she'd get a blessing."

"Is that the girl that-" Paul began, then remembered himself. "Uh, that, that let you go?"

"That's what he just said," said Kirk (or Jim).

I had practically been holding my breath. "Yeah. Uh, she said that we have to get out of here immediately. They're going to kill us."

"She said that?"

"Her words were 'you will die.'"

"We have to finish the raft soon," Grant said.

"Who's designing it?" I asked.

"Jim and Kirk are working on that part," Grant answered.

"We were both in construction," put in Jim (or Kirk), "for a while." In other words, the raft might sink once it hit the water.

"Who's going to tell Colin and the others in the valley what we're doing?" asked Jane. "They won't be too happy if we leave the island without them."

I held back a laugh at the picture.

"Maybe we'll grab some volunteers," Grant said dismissively. "How long do you guys think the raft will take to build?" he asked Kirk (and Jim).

"Depends," said Jim (or Kirk). "Most likely a week, if we start today."

We did start immediately after our powwow. The passengers started chopping down some trees and pulling the plane apart. They added it to the stuff we already had to build with. I helped in any way I could, mostly carrying logs.

That day, Day Sixteen, ended quickly. Even though we worked into late evening, using torchlights, we were worn out, and hadn't accomplished enough to keep up with the schedule.

As I laid down, using my travel bag as a lumpy pillow, I heard someone sit beside me.

"Hi," I said to whoever it was. I smelled coconuts. "Have you acquired the perfect tan yet?"

"Don't do that," said Dana tersely. "It's freaky. I'm not the only one catching rays. You're not pale any more either, you know."

"No, I didn't know. I'm probably bright red."

I heard her swallow uncomfortably. "I'm sorry."

I sat up. "For?"

"You know what for."

I was in complete shock, but I didn't let on. "What made you say that?"

"I thought you were dead. After what the natives did to those people yesterday...I though for sure they'd killed you."

Was it just yesterday? It seemed like a lifetime ago. "And...you cared?"

"I felt bad," she said correctively. "Because of what I'd said to you. I thought you were a wimp. But after you did all that hiking and running and escaping and stuff...I guess I was wrong."

I nodded. "Thank you." I considered telling her I had forgiven her right away, but that sounded cocky. "I forgive you, by the way."

"I don't like you or anything," she said quickly. "But I don't hate you."

"Can I ask you something, without you getting offended?" I said, swirling my finger in the sand. "Why don't you like me? Or anybody?"

"Nobody likes me." She sighed. "It's just hard. I had a bunch of people I thought were friends, but it was just because I was rich. And I had a really great boyfriend, but I found out he just dated me because he liked my money. I was never really pretty, before, and my 'friends' told me so. I had a really stupid life. And then my dad said I needed an attitude adjustment and sent me to a boarding school in England. He called me a few weeks ago and said he was sorry and wanted me back home. And now, I've gotten taller and thinned out and my hair is better and my skin is cleared up, and everybody at the boarding school says I'm hot, but I was just so…un-pretty before, and now I'm going back to L.A. to the same stupid friends, and I think the boarding school kids were just being nice…my L.A. friends are still going to think I'm ugly and they're still going to like me only for my money. Everybody's fake."

I let out a long breath. "Well…I'm not fake."

"You're not my friend."

"I could be…" I said quietly.

"I…guess my money won't do you much good."

"Right."

She was quiet for a while. "You won't tell anybody about what I said?"

I shook my head firmly.

"Okay, we can try being friends for a while. Just for a while."

"Okay." I tried smiling.

"That's nice," she said softly, the first time she didn't have an edge to her voice. "Your smile is nice," she repeated. "Good-night, jelly-fish."

"Good-night Barbie."

"Barbie?"

"Just guessing at what you look like."

"Hm," she said, laughing a little, and walked away.

Chapter 15

Days Seventeen through Twenty-three, the week in which we were supposed to build the raft, we worked long and hard, but still it was only halfway done.

The week went by very quickly, and nobody really had time to talk to one another. My arms ached from lifting lots of heavy materials, although I secretly hoped I was building up some kind of muscle. I knew I was getting more sun than I had in my entire life, although I doubted I had a tan. More of an all-over burn, most likely. I couldn't decided whether I should worry about what I looked like since I couldn't see myself, or whether I should just forget about it since I couldn't do anything about it anyway. Over all I decided to be indifferent.

I wasn't sure what we ate in that week, but I figured out someone was making some kind of stew with the meat we brought. I just ate it, along with a lot of fruit, and was thankful.

Day Twenty-Three dawned sunny and breezy, a good work-day. The passengers were trying to figure out how exactly to piece everything together with a very limited amount of screws and nails. Someone suggested first of all that we use wooden pegs, and second of all that we cut the logs in such a way they'll fit together tightly. Whoever that someone was, they were smart.

The problem was that we needed people who could carve the wood into correct shapes. Paul could, so that was one. We knew Karen and Zach could, but they were still in the valley. Those that had stayed there had apparently decided not to come back to the beach yet, and we needed to get this done.

A guy named Brad said he could carve fairly well, so that was two.

We were all standing around deciding if two was enough when Paul said, "Well, Rick is good at woodworking."

My head snapped up. "But-"

"You can do it, right Rick?" asked Grant. Why did he always have such faith that I could do things?

"Uhm...uh, see, I haven't carved since...well, I'm kind of...blind?"

"You can do it," Paul said convincingly. "It's just like learning to walk again."

I ran a hand through my hair.

"He might cut himself in half," someone pointed out.

"He's good," Paul said confidently. "He's really good. He won first place in a carving competition. He beat a thirty-year-old."

"Nineteen," I corrected, under my breath. "I...guess I could try. But if I lop a finger off or something, Paul, I'm blaming you."

"No probs. You won't."

"Fine. I'll do it."

I had to admit, it was scary handling a knife. Paul sat me down and positioned the wooden board I was carving between my knees. "Okay, three equally positioned notches, a finger-tip deep, starting here and ending here." He rubbed my finger over the marks he'd notched in the wood. "Got that?"

"Are you sure you need me to do this?"

"This is to start you out, man. It gets rougher. And we need somebody who isn't gonna make big gashes in the wood or uneven notches."

"How do you know I won't?"

"Your dad was a carpenter. It's gotta be in your blood. Plus, you're a very careful dude."

It took me quite a while, but I got the board done. Paul came over to inspect my work. "I can't believe this, dude. You're really good."

"Really?" I asked, my face lighting up.

"Super. Maybe it's better that you can't see it, that you can feel all the little imperfections. Wow. Here, I got more for you."

With each project I got a little less scared. I loved carving, more than I realized. If I could get really, really good at it maybe I could start my own business. I had Dad's tools already, and his knowledge. I could see a whole new future opening up for me. I never would have guessed I could go back to woodworking. It might be a bit impossible when it came to power saws, but...I'd work something out.

"Hey, dude," Paul said, coming back later. "You are so good. You look really happy. Practically giddy, actually."

"Thanks. I love this. It isn't much, but still."

"Uh, so, we're quittin' pretty soon, since it's getting dark."

"Is it? I guess it doesn't really matter to me. I can work late."

"Dude! You're like some kind of carpentry superhero. Although your fingers might get sore."

"Good point. Guess I can quit if you are."

"Yeah. Hey, uh, don't tell anybody that can't keep a secret, but you're carving circles around that Brad guy. He can't cut a straight notch."

"Wow."

"Seriously. And you're better than me."

I actually blushed. "I don't believe that."

"Yeah, well, you're pretty much good at everything you're not supposed to be good at anymore."

"I think it's just that I've been given the gift of determination."

"Amen to that."

"And stupidity, probably. I keep forgetting I'm not supposed to be doing any of this."

I was happier that day than I'd been in a very long time. Jane mentioned it when she sat by me at dinner. "The way you're working, you guys will have that stuff ready by the day after tomorrow."

"When are we going to go tell the people in the valley what we're doing? They probably think we're out here twiddling our thumbs, waiting for a plane."

"I didn't think Colin was going to – I didn't think Colin and the rest of the group were going to stay there this long."

I shrugged. "You miss Colin?"

"I miss all of them."

"But you miss Colin the most."

She sighed. "Grant is a really nice guy, but he can get exasperating. It was better when Colin was here to give everybody a down-to-earth perspective. Usually those two are fighting, because one is way out there at one end of the argument, and the other's way out there at the other end, and you and I have to get them to meet in the middle."

"Yeah. I miss those days. Grant hasn't had a good argument in a long time. He must be feeling purposeless."

"Rick!" Jane admonished, laughing. "Grant is really nice," she said again. "He's just trying too hard to make everybody happy here."

"I know. Poor dude. Does it scare you a little that he's the CIA guy that had to clear that mess up in England?"

"Yeah. I wonder what he'd do if he found out."

"Ground you. Or-"

She nudged me as someone came to sit by us. "Hi guys," said Grant.

I swallowed my stew too loudly.

"Hi Grant," answered Jane. She was trying not to laugh.

"Rick, great job with the carving. If you keep working on it, you could start a business back home."

"Thanks," I said, shoving fruit in my mouth to keep from laughing.

Grant clicked his tongue habitually. "What's so funny?" he asked good-naturedly.

"Nothing," Jane replied mildly. She changed the subject. "When are we going back to the valley?"

"Any time before the raft is done. Depends on who's going."

"Who's going on the raft or to tell the others we're building the raft?"

"Both. I'm not sure how we're deciding who's getting on the raft. One should, preferably, be Jim or Kirk, in case there's a structural problem while sailing. We've figured out we can probably get six people on it, with supplies."

"Are you going?" I asked. I didn't want him to. He was a good leader, and people listened to him better than anyone.

"Most likely. I'm the navigator."

"Oh," said Jane, very quietly. She didn't want him to go either, then. "Can I go?" she asked suddenly.

I raised my eyebrows but continued to eat, slowly.

"Well...I'd like you to come. I'm still not sure how we're deciding who's going. We could use that Bubble Gum rhyme," he added, laughing. It was nice to see - or hear, rather - him in a good mood. "I'd like Colin to stay here, on the beach, if possible."

"Oh," Jane said again.

"But I do want you to come." He sounded sincere.

"Uh..." Jane faltered. "I don't know. I mean, it might be all guys, and just me..."

"I'll protect you," he said kindly.

"Well," it sounded like she was smiling, "I'll think it out."

"Sure. Hey Rick, you want to come?"

"I don't know. It depends."

"On what?"

"On...who's going and who's staying."

"Who carries the swing vote?" asked Grant.

"It's not just one person." I was thinking of our main group: Grant, Jane, Colin, Paul and me. "I don't know," I repeated finally.

"That's okay," said Grant. "I was just seeing what everyone was thinking. Well, I have to go see a man about a sail." I heard him stand up. "See you later." He walked off.

"He never stops, does he?" I mused, finally finishing my meal.

"No," she sighed.

"When we were all sick, out there in the fields, and you went to get water, he wouldn't stop worrying about you. If something had happened to you, he'd blame himself forever."

"He cares about people a lot. I just hope nothing bad happens and he's left riddled with guilt."

I bit my lip. "What'll make you decide to go on the raft?"

"What'll make you decide?" she said, returning the challenge.

"Right." It all depended on who got on that raft. I didn't want to be stuck here with the Naturalists, but I wasn't the high-seas-adventure type either. "Well, it doesn't matter yet. I wonder if Colin will agree to stay on the beach," I said, yawning. "Omigosh!" I clamped a hand over my mouth in horror.

"What?!"

I let my hand off my mouth. "We didn't tell Colin and the others about the natives being here, about the rules for them not attacking us. What if the group decides to go exploring on the other side of the mountain?"

"Oh no! You don't think they'll do that, do you?"

"The professor seemed pretty pumped about the natives' encampment. And he's the exploring kind."

"Oh, please God, no." She sounded worried.

What are you thinking? Comfort the poor thing, you overbearing cynic! "I'm sure they'll stay put," I said quickly. "Colin's the safe sort. He'd make them stay in one place."

"We have to tell Grant." So saying, she ran away.

Please make them play it safe, I prayed. Please, please, please.

Day Twenty-four we sent out a team of four people to warn the group in the valley. I wasn't surprised that Jane was among them, first of all because she knew how to get there, second because she always seemed to be doing something exciting.

I didn't really care to go with them. I had carving to do. I carved the entire day until I was sure I had so many splinters in my fingers I had more wood on them than skin.

Paul came by to see how it was going. "We've pretty much got everything done."

I wiped sweat from my forehead. "How does the raft look so far?"

"Very two-dimensional. In the movies, it goes up in a flash."

I smiled and shook my head. "Films depicting survival are usually highly overrated."

"That right there sounded like something Prof. Taylor would say." I could picture him shaking his head at me. "So we're done for today."

"I just have to finish this up."

"Kay. See ya."

As I carved, someone sat beside me. I sniffed instinctively and caught the very faint coconut scent, which I was beginning to enjoy. "Where do you buy your tanning lotion?"

"I told you not to do that," Dana growled.

"You must be pretty bronzy by now."

"Stop making fun of me."

"I'm not. And if I were, I'd just be trying to even out the score."

"You're very sarcastic."

I smiled significantly. "What do you need?"

"I want to know how you do it. Are you crazy, is that it?"

I stopped carving. "What are you talking about?"

"You! Your – resolve...? You're like some kind of emotional rock. You do all these amazing things for a guy who can't even see, and everybody believes in you. I mean, you're part of the Inner Core, you know? You're one of the people who knows what's going on. What makes them like you?" She sure could talk.

I resumed carving. "I think the overall answer is that I'm stubborn. And I forget that I'm handicapped by anything - age, blindness, anything. And I have faith."

"In God?"

"Yeah."

"I'm supposed to be a Christian. I mean, we go to church and everything. And I'm saved, I guess. Or I was. Does it go away?"

Somehow her being a Christian didn't surprise me. "No, it can't go away if you don't want it to. Jesus died and rose again, so you can always be saved, it's whether you want to be saved that matters."

"Oh. Well...I want to. I didn't before, but I think I do now. I mean...I've tried praying again. So...what makes us different? Why isn't my faith the same as yours?"

"Do you believe God's out to get you? You know, one mistake on your part and that's the end, poof, you go to hell?"

"Kind of. Since my friends only liked me when I could do something for them, I guess I got a picture of God only liking me when I act a certain way."

"He said he's a friend that sticks closer than a brother. He's also our father. In my opinion that means he can forgive us for anything, as long as we want to be forgiven. I mean, I just talk to him like he's standing right next to me."

"I'm not used to that."

"Just talk. That's why he created us in the first place, so we could have a relationship with him. He's the only person who listened to me when I had problems."

She was quiet for a long time, and I finished my carving. "I need tweezers seriously bad," I said, rubbing my roughened fingers together.

"Oh, I carry some with me. Here, give me your hands." She started pulling the splinters out of one hand. I tried not to react to the stinging sensations. "Why do you want to be my friend?" Dana asked quietly.

I laid the plank of wood to the side with one hand. "Why not?"

"I'm mean and I'm not pretty and I'm a brat," she said in one breath.

"Well, I wouldn't care what you looked like even if I could see, and you haven't been particularly mean or bratty recently."

"It's...hard. My mom died when I was ten, and my dad married this lady I didn't know. She was nice, but I missed my mom. And, I never had any friends to talk to." She gave a harsh sigh. "But that's all so stupid to cry over when you lost your entire family and-"

"You still had something awful happen to you. Just because my problems seem worse doesn't make them any more important." I winced when she pulled out a deep splinter.

"It's just...when Mom died, there wasn't anybody to discuss how I felt about it. Dad tried to help me, but he was too sad to ever talk it out, you know? I just had to bottle it all up. You said your mom and dad died, didn't you? Was that before the airplane crash?"

"Yeah. I was twelve when it happened."

She started tweezing my other hand. "Who did you talk to?"

"God. He's the only one who was listening."

"Your brother died in the crash right? I heard he was the pilot."

"Yeah, Noah was the pilot."

"And there's nobody here to talk to about that, either."

"Except God, again." I waited a little while and then said, "You know, I'm your friend and all. You can talk to me about your mom."

"It happened nine years ago. You don't want to hear it."

"Why not? You want to talk about it. I never got what I wanted, and it tore me up inside."

"What did you want?" she asked, so quietly I almost didn't hear her. I could tell by the way she kept sniffing she was trying not to cry.

"Sympathy. I wanted somebody to care about what I was thinking. I don't think anybody knew I was so hurt. I don't think I even knew. I just realized a few days ago that what I wanted was to hug somebody and cry."

She sniffed. "I know."

"Judging by the way your dad asked you to come home, I think he's ready to talk about your mom now."

"I know," she repeated. "I just realized a second ago I want to go home. It's too bad you won't be there."

"Why?" I asked, slightly surprised.

"Why not?" she said, using my own answer on me. Her voice had changed slightly. It had lost most of its edge. I figured it would lose all the edge after she got home to her dad.

"I hope your 'friends' won't ruin everything for you."

"Maybe they won't," she said slowly. "I don't know." She sniffed and placed my de-splintered hands in my lap. "You won't ever get to hug somebody and cry, will you?"

I didn't care whether she felt sorry for me about that. "It doesn't matter anymore." Out of sudden curiosity I asked her, "Can I touch your face?"

"W-what?"

"I can tell what something looks like by feeling it. I'd kind of like to know what you look like."

"Okay." She took my hands and put it them on her cheeks. They were smooth and well-shaped, with high cheekbones. Her chin wasn't too long. Her nose was straight and came to a nice rounded point at the tip. Her ears were perfect. I felt her hair. It was smooth and healthy. "What color is it?" I asked.

"Light brown."

I felt near her eyes. The edges were wet, and a new tear spilled down.

"Why are you crying?" I asked with a smile, retracting my hands. "You're the first person I've seen with my hands. And you're beautiful."

She sniffed once again. "What?"

"I said you're beautiful. What color are your eyes?"

"Green."

"Wow. I was wrong. You're prettier than any Barbie."

"You're just saying that."

"Heck no," I scoffed. "I'm a blunt person. I wish I could see you for real."

She suddenly grabbed me in a hug and let go quickly. "I lied, before. I like you. You're my best friend." She kissed me on the tip of my nose, like I was a little boy, and left quickly, like she was too happy to stay put.

I rubbed my nose off on my arm. "Well," I said aloud to myself, "I was right. Girls like analytical short guys."

Chapter 16

Day Twenty-Five the passengers started nailing (pegging, mostly) everything together. It took all day to get the pieces together, but we worked quickly. By sundown, we surprised ourselves by finding that the only thing we needed to do was fit the mast and sail on, as well as load up the supplies. Again, nobody mentioned and I didn't ask what 'supplies' were. Probably a whole lot of fruit.

At the end of that day, everybody was pretty happy, although there was a little bit of tension because practically everybody wanted on the raft and nobody knew who was going.

I somehow ended up sitting next to Grant at dinner-time. "Hi," he said. "Thanks for getting all the wood ready for us."

"It was fun, actually." I took a swig of water. "Do you know who's going to be on the raft yet?"

"Jim and I are definitely going," he answered firmly. "Unfortunately I don't know about anyone else until the group from the valley gets here. I'd like Prof. Taylor to go. And Jane."

"Jane didn't sound too sure," I reminded him. I couldn't tell what she wanted to do.

"I wish she would."

Hmmm, I said to myself. *Wonder if he'd want her if he knew who she really was?* It was kind of confusing. Colin and Grant liked Jane, and Jane liked both of them. I wondered if any of them knew they liked each other. I smiled.

"What?" said Grant good naturedly.

"Nothing."

"Is there some inside joke I don't know about?" he asked curiously.

I bit into a mango and only shook my head.

"You're sneaky, Rick," said Grant. I heard him stand up. "See you later."

"Yeah," I said, waving at him with my spoon.

"Dude," said Paul, plunking down beside me, "I'm scared."

I took time to think about that. "You're not serious?"

"Totally. I said hello to Dana today, and she totally said hi back."

"Yeah, she's not all bad."

"What was *that?*" asked a shocked Paul. "All of a sudden 'she's not all bad'? Where did you get that? Are you secret buddies now?"

"It's not secret."

"What, what are you – are you, like, dating or what? What happened?"

"You don't have to be in love with a girl to like her," I told him. "She just needed somebody to talk to."

"My gosh, you have a way with people. First Jane, now her. What do you do, like, hypnotize 'em?"

I laughed. "I didn't do anything to Dana. Between her heavenly father and her earthly father she would have turned out nice anyway. I just sort of sped everything up. I didn't do anything," I repeated.

"She was working pretty hard this week. She didn't go tanning today, either. And she didn't yell at anybody."

"She's nice, really. She's pretty too."

"Oh, I know. She's always been downright beautiful."

"Hold your horses," I said laughingly. "I don't think she's your type."

"Shut up," he snorted. "'You don't have to love a girl to like her.'"

"You're in quite the mood."

"So are you. You should get stolen by natives more often. Does great things for your attitude. Or maybe it was the kiss."

I shoved him. "You should stop. I'll never be the dashing, dating guy. I'm everybody's little brother and I'll always be that way."

"So you'll never marry?"

"Yeah, I'll marry, but I'd like to wait about a decade before I consider it."

"I'm sorry, dude. I was just kidding. Well," he sighed, "so the Drama Queen is nicey-nicey now. Wow. I wonder what's next. Maybe I'll wake up and find out I'm asleep on the plane."

I laughed.

"Hey, it's now been proven," said Paul. "Anything is possible."

Day Twenty-Six came, and we were all excited. There was an electric charge in the air, and we were working like crazy to get the sail on. This required more work than was expected.

We needed to get fruit for the 'supplies,' so a few of us were sent by pairs into the woods (or jungle or whatever it was). By coincidence Grant paired Dana and I. I, of course, had the exhilarating job of carrying the fruit bag. It was a big duffel bag, and Dana would find fruit and throw it in, while I tagged along. These were the same woods Jane had found me in after I climbed out of the ravine.

"Are you going on the raft?" asked Dana.

"I don't know yet. Probably not."

"Really? I figured you'd talk to your friends and get on."

I tried to figure out whether she was being sarcastic once again. Probably not. "No. I just don't know yet." I didn't really want to go. There were a bunch of people who wanted on more than I did. "I think there are probably people better suited for a long, wet ride."

"I want to go."

"Oh. Why?"

"When we meet a ship, I want to send a message to my dad right away, to tell him I'm okay."

"Are you sure it's safe for you? I mean, you're a girl."

"I kind of know that."

"Well…it'll probably be all guys. Unless Jane goes."

"Are you sure she's going to get back here in time? When are we sailing?"

I shrugged.

"It's nice of you to want me to be safe," she said after a while. "Safety's a big issue right now. That's why we're in pairs, right?"

I took a moment to try and picture Dana and I fighting a bunch of natives. It didn't present a reassuring picture.

"You know, I could get Grant to give the message to your father. You can trust him."

"Is it really any safer here than on the raft?"

I paused. "I think it's about even. Maybe you're right. Maybe the raft is safer than being around here."

Somehow, in the moment between when I stopped talking and Dana started to answer me, I heard a birdcall. Something in my brain clicked.

I grabbed her arm. "Sh."

She went quiet. I heard the call again. I'd heard that call before, every time right before they showed up. It was different from the normal birdcalls I heard every day.

"Get down," I whispered. We crouched to the ground.

"What is it?" she asked, her voice just loud enough for me to hear.

"The natives." Or Naturalists. Or whatever they were.

We were about a mile from the beach, and the birdcall was coming from that direction. "Can you see anything?" I asked her.

"No. What should we do?" Her voice was shaking.

This poor girl. I was supposed to be playing the role of the dashing hero, and here I was, a mere boy, unable to see. What was a guy supposed to do in a situation like this? And then I figured that most guys I knew of weren't likely to be in my situation.

"We'll stay along the tree-line and head for the beach. I don't know what's going on, but there's strength in numbers."

"What about the other fruit-pickers?" she asked, concerned.

"Uh...you go find them. I'll stay here. But run like the wind, Dana."

She got them and returned to where I was. It turned out to be Paul and some guy named Greg.

I told them my plans for going back to the beach, and Paul said that seemed like the best idea.

We walked, crouched over, along the tree-line. Suddenly we stopped.

"Oh, my God, no," murmured Paul.

"What?" I asked.

"They're standing there behind the tree-line in view of the camp with a big – I dunno, some kind of machine, it looks like a big drum. This one guy has his hand on a lever..."

I heard a yell from the beach.

"Everybody, duck!" shouted Paul hoarsely.

We hit the ground just as a big explosion sounded from the direction of the beach. The ground shook. The experience was not unlike the 'fireworks' display we'd encountered before.

Afterwards there was a roaring sound coming from the beach, and people were shouting.

"They blew up the raft," Paul said, probably for my benefit. "They just...look at it. Look at that fire."

"It's gone," said Greg.

"They saw us," said Dana quickly. "Run!"

"Back to the woods, we can hide," ordered Paul.

Glad he took the leading man part, I though as I held onto his arm and we dashed for safety. That was a pretty stupid thing to think about.

I heard a whistling noise behind me. There was a grunt, and somebody fell. "Greg!" yelled Paul, releasing my arm.

"Leave him, Paul!" shouted Dana. "He's dead! Look at where he's shot!"

"Wait, just wait!" begged Paul.

Dana grabbed my arm and started running, and I followed her willingly. I heard Paul come up behind us.

There was another whistling noise. It sounded close. I braced myself. Dana fell, and I went with her. We slammed into the ground and she cried out in pain. "Dana!" I touched her face, scared she was dead.

"My leg," she said, crying.

Paul was right beside me. "It's okay, it's okay," he said. He wasn't exactly convincing. "I've got her. Run, Rick."

"You've got her? What-"

"I'll carry her! Run!"

"But she's-"

"Rick!"

"Go, Rick," sobbed Dana. "It's okay."

I ran, I wasn't exactly sure where, shielding my face with my arms in case I met up with any trees. I tried going in a straight line towards the woods. I felt my way through the trees, waving my hands in front of me. I tripped and fell numerous times, but adrenaline pushed me to go on. The last time I fell I landed near bushes. I crawled into them, hoping I was shielded enough to hide.

I listened. I could hear voices, faintly. I tried to pray but I was so scared and confused I couldn't think. *God*, was all my brain could come up with.

Footsteps. Very softly, as if it were a light person. I held my breath. I heard them move. "Rick?"

I knew they were looking at me. I could have pleaded for my life, but that wouldn't do much for me.

"Rick, it is I, Chloe."

I was almost relieved. I wasn't sure whether she'd have the brains enough to kill me.

"Don't speak," she said, crawling in beside me and sitting next to me. We sat in silence for a long time. "Alright, it's safe," she said finally.

"What's going on?" I asked angrily. "You people broke the rules – nobody went into your territory."

"You don't understand. You were leaving."

"You told me we had to leave!"

"Sssh! I was wrong. I didn't know that it was unfair."

"Un-unfair?!" I sputtered. "You were unfair! You guys blew up our raft!"

"But if you left then it wouldn't fulfill your destiny."

I considered slapping her to wake her up from her delusion. Maybe that would make her realize we weren't living in a fairytale. "Destiny? What is our destiny, Chloe?"

"All will be rev-"

"Don't you dare give me that," I said, grabbing her arm. "I am sick and tired of being scared of you people, without knowing what's going on. What are you going to do to us after a year?"

"The best of you will have survived," she recited.

"Yeah, I got that part. Then what? You kill us?"

"You will fight each other to the death. Then the winner will become our leader, to dispose of us as he or she will. We will accept our Fate."

I sat there, trying to figure out how this could make sense in some way. "Why are you people accepting this?"

"It was in a proverb. 'A sun's ray will fall to earth when your new Ruler is sent.' We welcomed you with a light display, do you remember?"

So that was what the fireworks were for. "I remember."

"The proverb goes on to explain that after a year, on the seventeenth day of the Golden Month, the best of the sun's servants will remain, and they will fight to the death for the Ruler's position. Then all will fall into place as the Ruler sees fit."

"You do realize that this is extremely hokey."

She seemed shocked. "You don't believe me? What is hokey?"

"Stupid," I said simply. "We came on an airplane, Chloe. We make airplanes. It came from England, where your ancestors are from. It's like a big ship that can fly. We were blown off course and crashed here, not on purpose. And none of us will ever kill each other."

"You don't know you were sent here? The proverb mentions no knowledge on the servants' part," she mused.

"Look, did you take our transmitter? Was it because you don't want us off the island?"

"What is a transmitter?"

"Did you take anything from us?"

"Yes. We took some of your food supply to see what you ate. We also took many devices which transmit power."

"Did you cut a flap in the side of the plane to take a device?"

"Yes. It was to keep you from finding a way off of the island."

That was why they'd taken all the electronics. It wasn't a crazy person who was stealing, it was the natives, preventing us from getting home. I laughed bitterly. "So we're going to die any way we look at it. I suppose if a rescue plane came you'd blast it out of the sky."

"I'm sorry, Rick." She sounded genuine. "I don't think you were meant to die," she said for the second time. "But I'm afraid you will."

"None of the passengers will kill me," I told her.

"My people have gone," she said softly. "I must go with them." She took my hand and led me out of the bushes. "When the time comes, I will speak for you." She kissed my hand and left.

Chapter 17

"Spooky," said a voice. It was Paul. He was standing behind me. He came over and grabbed me in a hug. "I'm so glad you're alive."

"How long were you standing there?"

"Long enough to see Little Ghost Girl kiss you. On the hand. I s'pose that's the same girl you told me about before?"

"Yeah." I stepped out of his hug and rubbed a hand over my face.

"What's wrong, dude? What'd she say?"

"I'll tell you later. How's Dana?"

"She'll be okay. The arrow went into her calf. It didn't go in that deep."

"Is that Greg guy still alive?"

"No. He was shot through the neck."

I grimaced and shivered.

"It's bad, isn't it?" he said. "What she said to you, it's bad."

I sighed deeply, my voice shaking. "We can't get off the island." He didn't answer me. "Why did you call Chloe Ghost Girl?"

"She's thin and extremely pale. She has white-blonde hair and dark eyes and was wearing a white dress. Horror-movie kind of thing...I think we are in a horror movie." He changed the subject. "We should go back to the beach. I found the bags of fruit, can you carry them?"

I nodded. Paul's voice had changed. It was lower, much sadder, than usual.

Not that I could blame him. Our entire hope for survival had just been blown to tiny pieces, literally. We weren't getting off of this island. Not alive. I didn't know exactly how to take that.

Dana was waiting for us by the fruit. She had stopped crying, although I wouldn't blame her if she hadn't. She was tougher than I thought. "Hi," she said to me. "Glad you're okay."

"Are you okay?" I asked.

"Nothing a little plastic surgery won't take care of later on." She was joking, I knew, but I couldn't laugh at it, I couldn't even smile. Plastic surgery...only back in the real world. And we weren't going back to the real world.

"Rick." Paul put a hand on my arm. "It'll be okay."

"What...what are you talking about?" asked Dana slowly.

"One of the natives...Chloe," I began, "she's the one that let me go the first time. I met her again a few minutes ago. She told me what they were planning for us. Dana, we're not getting off this island."

She made a choking noise. "B-but – Rick, are you just being a cynic again?"

"No," I said, very strongly. "This is the truth."

She sniffed. "I-I don't think I can make it here any longer." She started crying quietly.

"Dana," said Paul gently. "Hey, hey, look at me. There's only one thing we can do now. That's just live. Here. Like it's our new home. For a year, we can live like we're kings – and queens - of this island." He was starting to sound like Paul again. "We can swim in the ocean, we can explore, we can build those funny little, like, hut things like in the movies-"

Dana snorted with laughter. "I know what Rick's thinking: We can tan," she said, laughing at me, and Paul joined her.

I shook my head. "We can make fun of me all day..." I said, continuing the list.

"Can you do that?" Paul asked her. "Can you live like it's the best year of your life and not your last?"

"It's stupid," she said roughly.

"It's survival," I corrected.

"Sure," she sighed. "I can do it. If you fix my leg first. It hurts really bad." She was a lot tougher than I could have ever imagined.

I carried the fruit, and Paul carried Dana, and we headed back to the beach. Though the fire had probably lost its fury, I could still hear the raft burning.

"Thank God!" Grant shouted, coming up to us. "We were just going to send somebody to find you." He sounded exhausted. I wondered how bad this was affecting him right now.

"We need to talk. Right now," I said forcefully. We went off to an area apart from everyone, where it was quiet. "I have bad news," I started.

I told him what Chloe said. He didn't respond. I could picture his face; grim, devoid of the handsomeness Paul said he had. The poor guy. In some way he felt like he hadn't protected us enough. "One year," he said, emotionless.

"Grant...Paul talked to Dana and me about this. He had a really good point. There's nothing you can do, that any of us can do, to get out of here. All we can do is live, for a year, like this is our home."

"I...I didn't think they'd keep us here..." He was struggling to accept the fact that he couldn't find a solution to get us out of here.

"Grant." I reached out to touch his shoulder. He suddenly seemed too young, even to me, to have to handle guilt like this. "You can't save us, Grant."

"I couldn't save Peter, either," he said gravely. Somehow I knew he meant his friend that died in the car crash. Maybe this was why he felt he had to save people, that everybody was his responsibility.

There was something that happened in that car crash, some awful moment, that made Grant the way he was. It reminded me of Jane losing her fiancé. There was something about seeing their loved-ones die that only they could know about. I realized that even though Mom and Dad had passed away, at least I didn't have to see their suffering.

"You can't save us in the way you think," I said. "But you can go out there and tell them what Paul told me: All we can do is live."

"You're young, for being so smart," he said, and he might have been smiling at me.

"So are you," I answered. "Go."

He went. I didn't follow him. I sat down on the sand. *God? You have to help these people. They have families that are waiting for them back home. These people are not going to take this very well. Please, let them find happiness, sometime.*

And help me. I don't want to be stuck on this stupid island for the rest of my life. I don't want to die in a year, especially not by the hands of the natives. Help me make it through this, if only day-by-day. I'm relying on you. You must have a plan.

For about two days after that, everybody was walking around in a sort of trance. Nobody really knew what to do, how exactly they were supposed to live out their time on the island.

Grant was in pretty bad shape. Eight people, those working on or close to the raft at the time, died in the explosion, and a few people were injured. Everybody came to Grant for encouragement, and he gave it to them. I knew he'd come through this alright, but he felt like he wasn't giving these people what they needed. He told me so, once in a while, in his own words. Right now I was the only person he'd really talk to, and I was never sure why, although I was honored that he did. Grant seemed very human these days, not the usual Superman that I was used to.

I sat by Grant at lunch on Day Twenty Eight. I still didn't know what I was eating, and I still didn't care. "Hi," I said to him.

"Hi, Rick. What are you up to?"

"Clearing up the pieces of what used to be the raft." Everybody was. Most of it made good campfire material.

"I wonder if the group from the valley will come back soon?" he wondered, and I couldn't tell if he was looking forward to it. "They'll be in for quite a shock."

I hadn't thought about breaking the news to them. "I'll tell them," I said firmly. "You don't have to."

"Thank you," he sighed in relief. "I'll be glad Colin when comes back. We have a lot of injured people now. I'll feel better once he looks them over." He was sounding a little bit better now than usual.

"Grant…is that your first name?" I asked curiously. I'd been meaning to find out for a while now.

"No," he said, sounding surprised. "My name is Michael. Michael Grant."

"Michael's a nice name. How come all you CIA people usually go by your last name only?"

He paused. "We do?"

"On TV you do."

He chuckled. "Uh, don't believe everything you see about CIA guys on TV."

"I'll remember that. Then again, come to think of it, I won't be seeing much TV anymore. Not that I watched it that much anyway, but I was kind of looking forward to the season finale of St. Aidan."

"Yeah, I liked that show," said (Michael) Grant. "I was wondering whether Jack died or not. Hope not."

"Well, I don't know. Did you like him or James better? I thought Jack was kind of weird."

"I don't know."

"I was kind of hoping Shannon might get bumped off. She's so about The Drama," I said, making little quotations with my fingers.

He actually laughed. "Thanks, Rick."

"What for?"

"Being a funny kid." I heard him stand up. "I have to go talk to somebody. See you later."

"Bye."

I asked Paul to let me know when the valley group got here. It was later in the afternoon that he came to get me. "They're back," he said excitedly. "Everybody's really happy to see them. They're all, like, practically jumping on 'em."

"Where's Grant?"

"I dunno."

I asked everybody for a moment to talk to the newly arrived group, and the rest of the passengers seemed to understand what I was going to tell them.

"What the devil's going on?" asked Darby characteristically.

"We had...a problem."

"Where is Grant?" asked Jane.

"He's around. Just let me talk to you first. It's going to be kind of hard to tell, so please, just listen to me."

I told them, in so many words, that we had a year left. I gave them the 'We Must Go On' speech, trying not to sound too hokey. They were pretty quiet when I was done. I heard them shuffling around, somebody sniffing.

"Well, who'd have thought we would end up this way?" said Darby softly.

They broke off, one by one. Prof. Taylor patted me on the shoulder. "It's not as bad as it seems. Maybe those people are right. Perhaps we were meant to lead them."

As he walked away, I had a bad feeling come over me. I shook it off. "Rick, how's Grant taking it?" Jane asked.

"The way we expected. Everybody's taking it hard. And everybody will be okay. But, you should talk to Grant."

"Me?"

I nodded. "I don't know if you understand, but he – I think now would be the time to take him aside, tell him about...you."

She pulled in a breath, as if preparing herself. "Okay." She went away.

"Rick," said Colin in somewhat of a greeting. "What, uh, what did you mean just now? About Jane? I wasn't – I wasn't listening or anyfing, I just-"

"You have to ask her."

"Sure."

"Would it be okay if you, you know, took over for a while? For Grant? You don't know what it's like to be in charge of all these people all the time."

"No," he said, in a way that defied argument.

I nodded. "Just out of curiosity, why not?" I asked, defying. "What makes you the opposite of Grant?"

"Rick..." He sighed. "I have to help the injured, the sick, the dying – if I had to take care of the healfy people too, I couldn't handle it. I deal wif death constantly in medicine. I can't care about people like Grant can. If I did, I would be weighed down under guilt every day, and I couldn't be a help to anybody."

"You're a doctor. You have to care about people."

"It's not the same. I can care enough to fix 'em, I can't care enough that when they die I cry over 'em."

I paused effectively. "That's not going to work out here."

He made a confused sound. "What?"

"We have one year here, Colin. We are spending one year in one place with the same people. You are going to end up caring for these people, and some of us are not going to make it. What if it were Jane? What if she dies? You didn't know her from anybody when we crashed here, but you've spent time with her. You can't help caring for her. It's not a bad thing, it just happens. You can try and convince yourself you don't like her, but when she dies you're going to be sorry you didn't get to know her better."

"That doesn't have anyfin' to do wif leading these people," he said, his voice even deeper than usual.

"Yes, it does. They want you to help them, because you know how to help people. You just don't want to get attached to them."

"They're not my responsibility."

I shook my head. "Is that how you see it? If you don't care about them, you don't have to be hurt when they leave you? Did you decide not to care about your dad 'cause he left you, and you thought it wouldn't hurt if you didn't care?"

There was a long pause, in which I wondered if he'd walked away. Finally he whispered, "How do you figure these things out?"

"That's what you're doing, Colin. You're doing it to everybody." So ended my sermon. I wondered what he thought of me, a kid, telling him off.

He sighed a few times, like he was trying to say something. "Why did you use Jane as an example?"

I bit the inside of my cheek. "Cause you care about her."

He sighed again. "You are uncanny, Rick. You have the gift of seeing people from the inside-out." He put a hand on my shoulder. It was a big, heavy hand, with long fingers. "I fink Grant deserves some rest, how 'bout you?"

I tilted my head up to smile towards him. He tweaked my nose and walked away.

I found my way over to Dana, who was recuperating. "How's it going?" I asked, standing next to her.

"Wish that big doctor guy would get over here. Although whoever the temp doctor was, they fixed it pretty well."

"'Big doctor guy,'" I repeated, smiling amusedly.

"He's a hunk, actually," she informed me.

"Actually," I said, leaning against the tree she was sitting by, "he's a hunk who's an intern."

"How do you do that?" she asked, in some kind of awe.

"What?"

"Just…you standing there, you look like you're some kind of…adult. And I saw you talking to all those people from the valley, and to the doct- intern later. They listen to you like you're one of them."

I knelt next to her. "It's not always the greatest thing, being…old."

She didn't speak for a while. "I guess you can't go back to being a kid, once you're old."

"No," I said regretfully. "But I don't really care." I smiled at her.

"Sometimes, you do look like a kid. Sometimes, when you smile."

I sat down and leaned against the same tree, drawing my knees up to my chest. We sat there for a while, listening to the birds and the waves, the campfires crackling. Somebody started strumming a guitar.

I yawned peacefully. "Is that Paul playing?"

"Yeah," she replied, sighing sleepily. "It starts today, you know," she said indifferently. "Our time limit."

Somebody laughed. The breeze off the ocean rustled the leaves above my head. These were all the sounds I would become used to over the period we lived here. These were the sounds of my new home.

Chapter 18

Day Three Hundred and Ninety Two I found myself in much the same sentiment as a year ago.

So many things had happened in the year we lived on the island.

The number of passengers had gone from forty right after we crashed, to twenty-one at the beginning of our time limit. Since then one died in a winter storm, two died in separate hunting accidents, six died of illness. That left twelve of us.

In our year, we had built houses in the grass fields. They were huts, really, but they were much better than sleeping under a tree. I helped build them, using my ever evolving woodworking skills. I was thankful that I had such a handy talent. I couldn't make anything fancy, but I did what I could. We built four huts, two for the boys and two for the girls, having to split a few married couples. Those rough little piles of sticks were our homes, and we eventually thought of them as that.

We were organized. We had cooking shifts, watch shifts, hunting shifts, and washing shifts. Paul and I sort of got out of some of it, because we were the furniture builders. Even though we were in the middle of nowhere, we had furniture. I'd cut most of it, and Paul would piece it together. Eventually I figured out how to feel out and carve basic designs, which probably looked silly in the huts. We had tables and chairs, and once we made a dresser.

There were exploring trips for people who hadn't got to check out the island, but after a while we were used to all of it. I couldn't exactly walk off somewhere by myself, but I could get around our main camp area pretty well with my walking stick.

There were two weddings performed by a guy named Doug, who was somehow ordained by the Save the Whales program (we just decided it was legal). A couple named John and Christie, both of whom died later from cholera, and Zach and Karen.

A few people, including Paul and Dana, were kind of dating. Those two got along together in a weird, sort of joking way. I didn't really understand them.

One person I was surprised not to see (or hear) get together with anyone was Jane. She got very close to both Grant and Colin, but I never could tell which one she liked better. Apparently they couldn't tell either, because neither one of them made any serious commitments to her. Maybe she wanted it that way. I didn't know.

I didn't change, living this way, as much as I had when we first got there. Not on the inside, anyway. Paul said I had a pretty nice tan (then again, we probably all did now), I was at least two inches taller, and I was pretty fit looking. Ironically, by then, I didn't care. We were all on rations, which was better for weight loss than any diet back in the real world. Paul said we were all pretty thin and in fairly good shape, as far as physique went. But our health was failing. We weren't used to living like this, and it was taking its toll.

Cholera hit half the group at the one-third point in our year, but eventually all but four recovered. Two other people died later from pneumonia.

The storm, or monsoon, which happened in the winter season, not only destroyed our huts, but killed one man.

Two people died in hunting accidents. One was gored by a wild pig and the other shot himself accidentally.

These events, and learning to live in the harsh environment, had made the rest of us not only stronger, but closer to each other. We realized the value of each person. We were all one big group of friends, who usually got along, but nature allowed for a fight once in a while. We weren't grim or cynical, like we thought we'd be after going through all of this. We were the same. It was just that now we were all survival super-heroes. We did things we would have done in the 'real world' (as we always referred to civilization). We played games, we had a 'luau' at Christmas, and we had inside jokes with each other. We were too civilized to change much.

As we neared the end of our time limit, no one started panicking, no one started to become emotional. We knew death was coming, yet somewhere in our hearts we had a tiny glimmer of hope that something miraculous would happen and we'd be saved.

Day Three Hundred Ninety Two, three hundred and sixty four days since our year's time limit began, we went on with our lives as usual. There was going to be a kind of farewell party to each other at dinner that night, with some sort of island fruitcake, but that was as far as we were going towards feeling sorry for ourselves.

Late that afternoon, just before dinner, I was sitting outside my hut, leaning against it, slightly unaware I was in the same position I had been a year ago.

"You haven't changed much," said Dana, sitting beside me.

"What do you mean?"

"You always sort of move around in the background, knowing everybody and everything but not saying anything."

"Oh, that." I smiled. "Nobody here has changed that much. Not really. Not their character. You, for instance, are still a spoiled little L.A. girl."

"Rick!"

"Colin told me you had a manicure yesterday from Gale." Gale was a manicure/pedicurist in the real world. That experience didn't help her much here, although living on a farm when she was little did.

"That's funny, Rick. Funny. Actually she was getting a splinter out of my hand. And what have you been doing lately? Carving a little box. What exactly is someone going to do with a jewelry box?"

"Hey, you weren't supposed to know about that," I said, slightly upset. Paul wanted me to carve it for her. She wasn't supposed to know it was his idea, but keeping secrets around these people wasn't easy. I gave up. "Your boyfriend was going to put it together," I told her.

"Paul is not my boyfriend," she said. Even after all this time, there was edge to her voice that came in when she was mad.

"Dana, when there are only twelve people living in very close proximity to each other, things like manicures and boyfriends are hard to hide."

"Rick, you never stop teasing me, do you?"

"You're easy to tease."

"You're easy to lose." She stood up and messed up my hair, a habit she'd started when she wanted to annoy me. "Bye."

I combed my fingers through my hair.

"Hi," said Jane, dropping down next to me.

"My second visitor," I said cheerily. "Boy, what a day."

"Still sarcastic," she said reproachfully.

I sighed. "We're pretty reminiscent today." We sat quietly for a while, like we were having a conversation in our heads. Neither of us was going to mention why we were being reminiscent. "Can I ask you something?" I started quietly.

"Yeah."

"Is it Grant or Colin?" I asked bluntly.

She hesitated. "If I said I didn't know what you were talking about, you wouldn't believe me."

"No."

"I'll say it anyway. I don't know what you're talking about, Rick."

I shook my head. "I don't know how you do it."

"What?"

"I can't keep a small thing like a jewelry box a secret, and after a year I still don't know who you like more."

"Do I have to like one of them more?" she queried. Was she smiling at me?

"No," I laughed. "You confuse me, Jane."

"I know." Obviously she wanted to be confusing. Maybe it was some inner spy mentality that made her keep me in the dark about things. "Who do you think I like more?" she challenged.

I considered.

Grant hadn't treated her that much differently since she told him who she was. He had avoided her for a while, like he wasn't sure what to do with her, but eventually he went back to being around her. Somehow, I figured he suspected she was the spy all along. He was smarter than some people gave him credit for.

He learned not to be guilty for everything bad that happened. He was still serious, of course, and still our leader. He talked to me a lot, and he got along with Colin better.

Colin had become more responsible. I knew my little talk to him had made him change his mind about things, and he treated me a little different after that. He respected me more. Other than that, he was the same. He tried not to argue with Grant, at least not to his face, although sometimes he'd tell me what he thought of Grant. "A nice guy, but he's all mushy and old-school." I had no idea what that meant, but Colin did call Grant his friend, and vice versa.

As for Jane, she was exactly the same. She was still in the middle of anything exciting and she was still mysterious.

"I don't know," I sighed.

"I don't, either."

I didn't quite believe her. I changed the subject. "Did you want something?"

"Yes. Vincent asked if you could make him another cooking spoon."

"Cooking spoon? He broke another one?" I wouldn't have put it past him. Vincent was a big guy (according to Paul) and very strong. He had been a cowboy.

"He's on KP, with Gale and Zach. Actually, Colin broke the extra spoon yesterday. He stepped on it."

"They want me to make another one, huh? What, right now? Do they think I just say Abracadabra and poof, there's a spoon?"

"I don't think they want it right away," she said, laughing.

I paused. It didn't exactly make sense to start working on a spoon that wouldn't be finished for a while, and a spoon we wouldn't use.

"I know what you're thinking," she said quietly. "It's just a spoon. We're all going around doing things like tomorrow's just another day."

"Fine." I nodded. "It's just a spoon. I'll talk to Paul. Where is he? Oh, shoot. I have to tell him I spilled the beans about the box...you can't keep anything quiet around here," I grumbled.

"Not much. I'll take you to Paul." She took my hand and helped me up. "You've gotten taller," she told me.

"Fruit stew make me strong like bull," I said in a Jolly Green Giant voice.

Paul was hard to find. Turned out he was finishing up Dana's jewelry box. Jane said she'd see me later.

"Sup?" Paul asked in a partially distracted voice.

"I have to get materials to make a spoon."

"Did Vince break another one? That dude has seriously doesn't know his own strength."

"No. Colin broke this one."

"Uh, is making a spoon now really...like, necessary?"

This whole spoon thing was making me feel apprehensive about the next day. It's only a utensil, I said to myself. I told Paul so.

"Everybody's bein' really brave, but you know what we're all thinking," Paul whispered.

"Paul..." I bit my lip. I didn't want to get mushy on him, but he'd done a lot for me and I should let him know I appreciated it. "Thanks," was all I said. I knew he'd understand what I meant.

"You too, dude. You've been cool." I could tell by his voice he was smiling.

"Oh..." I grimaced. "Well, I haven't been too cool recently...Dana knows about the box."

"What?"

"Why are you giving it to her?"

He started to talk and stopped, then started again. "I like her."

"Yes, we all know that. But a jewelry box?"

"It seems pointless, I know. But remember when she told you and me about her mom's jewelry box that got lost in the crash?"

Dana was more sentimental than I first thought. She'd said she really wished she hadn't lost that box. "That is pretty cool of you. It's a nice farewell gift…"

"Yeah. You know…if we had more time, I think I'd marry her."

I nodded, not exactly surprised. "Time. The most important thing we don't have."

"No, the most important thing we don't have is a helicopter."

A smile creased my face, slowly. "Do you think Jane would marry Grant or Colin?"

He sniffed. "Hard to tell. She's mysterious. Some guys like mysterious women."

I snorted. "That's stupid. Her mysteriousness is driving me nuts."

"I know. I was just saying. It's only in the movies, you know."

"Most things in movies are completely unrealistic, once you think about it." I stood up.

"So, we can use some wood pieces I've got laying around for the spoon. We can start, like, after dinner if that's cool."

"Cool." I did a thumbs-up. A spoon we don't need. It was pretty stupid to worry over. Amazing what can upset someone.

At dinner, ten of us gathered around the big fire pit to eat. Darby and Karen weren't joining us, because they were sick with another bout of cholera.

To tell the truth, we were surprised Darby had made it this long. He was so stubborn, he'd somehow survived. He was still the same rude and abrasive English brat. Not that you could tell when he was so sick he couldn't talk.

Our meal consisted of the usual rations for the main course, then for dessert the KP crew presented their spectacular fruit cake. I never liked fruit cake, but this one was a hundred times better than any store bought thing I'd had.

After that, we stood up and toasted each other in some way, mostly using inside jokes and making fun of things. I didn't know what I was going to say when I stood up, and I mentioned it to them. At least that got a laugh. "Uh...obviously I'm not a professional public speaker." I played with the cap of my water bottle. "I'll make this short. I'd like to say thank you to Vincent for being a hilarious guy that always makes us laugh, to Gale for being really sweet and helpful, and...this sort of sounds like an Emmys speech..." They laughed. "Um, and to Darby, who's not here, for being somebody we can argue with when we're in bad mood. To Karen, who also isn't here, for being a tomboy who taught me how to climb. To Dana, my very good friend, who forgives me when I tease her. To Paul, the coolest dude ever, for... being the coolest dude ever. To Prof. Taylor, who tells us what we're doing wrong so we can fix it." They snickered. "To Grant, for dealing with us all the time and not losing his mind. To Colin, who saved my life. And to Jane, who saved me from going crazy." I shuffled back and forth. "And I'd like to thank all of you for treating me like an equal. I'm glad I got to grow up around you guys. I'd never have made it to fifteen without you." It was probably the first time I'd referred to my being a kid. I sat down, and blushed profusely when they clapped.

Grant was the last person to go, but his toast was the best. "I can't thank you all enough for putting up with me, and letting me put up with you. I know you think of me as your leader, and that is the highest honor I have ever received." This meant a lot when we thought about all the CIA awards he'd been given. "You are the closest family I've ever had. I am humbled by you – your perseverance, your dedication to helping each other, and your constant positive attitude have made me proud to be here with you. Thank you." We clapped, cheered, and I think somebody was crying. Grant deserved to be cried for.

After the clapping died down, we all sat quietly for a while. Vincent, with his slow drawl, gave one extra toast. "To all our friends who died. And to us, who are goin' to see them soon. It'll be better up there with them, anyway. Good-bye, all."

"Good-bye," we repeated. There was something in all of our voices that showed we weren't quite ready to leave each other yet. We were holding on to one hope - we'd get out of here. We wouldn't let go until we died.

Chapter 19

Day Three Hundred Ninety Three began like every other normal day on the island. It was sunny and warm, but with a refreshing breeze off the ocean.

I was still working on that dreadful spoon. I was absorbed in my thoughts of the past year. Through everything, somehow I'd come out alright overall. How? That's what I wanted to know. How had any of us survived this year?

By the Grace of God, that was the only possible answer. He'd had my back the whole time.

I took a moment to gather these thoughts and decide how I felt about dying. I was still only fifteen years old. I was talented, God had given me that. I hadn't always gotten everything I wanted, although I usually got what I needed. I had friends here, good, close friends that I didn't want to have to part with. Then again, maybe God had reached them and I'd see them in heaven. I had shared my faith with them, and I was a walking miracle; maybe I'd made more progress with them than I thought.

Did I want to die? No. Was I okay with dying? I'd try pretty hard to keep living, but I couldn't help looking forward to a better life with God than here on earth with all its problems. Yes, I was okay. Peaceful, actually. I would be a little scared when the natives came, but deep in my heart I would be at peace with whatever happened.

"And the philosopher sits philosophizing while the rest of us toil away." I jumped at Colin's voice. "You wanna help a poor guy out? I've got to go get drinking water and Paul's abandoned me and gone off who knows where."

I figured Paul was probably with Dana. "Sure." I set down my tools and extended a hand. He pulled me up easily.

We were headed away from camp, backpacks full of empty water bottles, when Colin grabbed my arm, stopping me dead.

"What?" I gasped.

"They're here."

I didn't have to ask who 'they' were. He guided me quickly back to camp, where he told Jane they were coming. "They're just coming out'f the forest now."

"Oh." Her voice shook a little. "Colin…"

"What happened?" asked Gale as she came up.

"They're here," said Colin quickly. "I'm going to find Paul-"

"Dana's with him," I said confidently.

"Be back," he said, leaving.

"I'll get Vince and the Professor," Gale offered.

"I just saw Grant and Zach, I'll get them," replied Jane. "Rick, get to Darby and Karen and tell them."

I obeyed. We were being fairly calm at the moment, considering the natives weren't more than a mile away from us. I knew the camp well enough to find the tent in which we housed the sick. I pulled back the flap and went in. "Anybody awake?" I asked gently.

"Karen's out," said Darby hoarsely. "What's up?"

"They're coming."

"What'm I supposed to do? Grab a gun and crawl out onto the field?"

I grinned. "You never stop, do you? I think Grant's going to tell them you're sick, and you can just stay here."

"And get slaughtered lying down? Hardly." I heard him moving. "I'll get it sitting up." He coughed.

I started to leave.

"Rick."

"Hm?"

"You're a good kid," he whispered. "I'm sorry."

I swallowed. I knew he wasn't sorry for one thing in particular. He was saying it to all of us. "We like you more than you think, you know."

"I know."

"Bye." I left and went back to the center of camp.

As I did so, I heard a weird noise. It was like a low, rhythmic hum. "What are they doing?" I asked anyone who might be standing there.

"Chanting," Vince answered. He spat. "We're all here," he added informatively.

"Is Karen awake?" asked Zach.

I shook my head. "Darby was, though. He, uh...said sorry. He said..." I ran a hand through my hair.

"What for?" asked Vince.

"You have to understand Darby," said Jane quietly.

Grant clicked his tongue. "Hmm."

"What are we going to do when they get here?" Gale asked. "I mean, aren't we supposed to fight each other?"

"We'll play it by ear," Grant answered.

"You do the talkin', Boss," encouraged Vince.

Prof. Taylor, who rarely spoke, said: "Has anyone considered that the Naturalists might have a point?"

There was a long pause. "Come again?" Colin said harshly.

This was what I had been worried about. Taylor was the kind of guy that could go behind our backs.

"What if we are here to lead them?"

"Dear God," muttered Jane.

"No, we weren't sent here by a Divinity," continued Taylor, "but we have the ability to lead them. We can show them how to use their machines to serve better purposes. Their religion is fascinating. Intriguing, in fact."

"Whose side are you on?" challenged Vince.

Grant's tone was on the border of icy: "Are you going to kill all of us, Taylor?"

"I am merely saying, what if we could convince them we are their rightful leaders?"

"No." Grant was firm. "No. They are set in their ways, and the only way for one of us to be their leader is for the rest of us to die."

"Unless we all submitted to one of us. Would that work?" Jane asked Grant.

"It might..." he said very slowly. "Like I said, we'll have to play it by ear. We won't know what route to take 'til they get here."

"But Jane and I do have a point," clarified Prof. Taylor.

"Could be."

"What'll happen to Karen and Darby?" asked Zach.

"They'll probably be left out of this," answered Grant.

I could hear the natives (or Naturalists) getting closer. We all stood waiting for them. Paul stood next to me. "I'm right here, dude."

I smiled slightly.

They came up, chanting something about the elements - earth, water, fire, wind - something like that. It sounded like there were quite a few of them.

"Greetings from our people!" boomed the voice of their chief, Theodoric. I wondered how he felt about one of us taking his place. "Our scouts tell us there are two of you sick. Are they not joining us?"

"No," said Grant. "They'll have no part in this."

"We shall see," said Theodoric. "We honor you on this occasion..." He went on for quite a while babbling about the sun and destiny and things like that. Finally he said, "Are you ready, Servants of the Sun?"

"For what exactly?" asked Grant.

"You will battle on the top of Mount Leopold. Only one of you can win."

"There is no need for that," spoke up Jane. "We've already chosen a leader."

"No," Theodoric said with finality. "The proverb clearly states that they will 'fight to the death.'"

"Those are the exact words?" Grant asked.

"The exact," replied Theodoric. "All of you must fight. Even the injured."

"Don't be ridiculous," Grant scoffed. "They can't even stand on their own."

"Then they will easily be picked off, and the better opportunity for the rest of you to win."

They tied our hands behind our backs and immediately started to lead us away from our camp. "Any rules of play?" Grant called.

"No," answered Theodoric.

"What about weapons?"

"Whatever you can find."

We had a three-day journey ahead of us. We weren't supposed to speak to each other, although they let Paul describe things to me once in a while. He always spoke in a low voice, so they couldn't hear him well in case they decided he was talking too much.

I wasn't sure where we were most of the time, although it felt like we were going around the larger part of the mountain range and crossing over the foothills. Paul confirmed that later. He also said they were carrying poor Karen and Darby around on stretchers.

We were in unfamiliar territory after that. We were walking through grass fields after the foothills. Then we got close to the ocean. We went over a bridge, which had to be lowered from the other side. It was all literally uphill from there. Paul described the area surrounding us in a few words: "Mountainous, with lots of trees and little waterfalls. Like the pictures of jungles you see in calendars."

After getting through the rocky country, we stopped to rest in their village. When we got there, Paul started telling me what it looked like. "Dude, their houses are like mansions! They're built out of wood, but they must have figured out how to make glass, 'cause they got windows. Some of 'em are kind of built up into the trees. It's all sort of intertwined. There are some pieces of whatever ship they came in. And the figure-head, some kind of angel or something, is sitting in the middle of town."

"A water sprite," said a girl, coming up to us. "She guards us." I knew it was Chloe. It had to be.

"Hi there," I said quietly. "You've changed. I mean, your voice is a little different." It wasn't as little-girly anymore.

"You're amazing," she breathed. "I am different. I'm quite taller. And so are you, I see. You've gotten to be quite-"

"Chloe!" someone called sharply. "Stay away from them. You must not disturb them."

"Good-bye, my hero," she said a little loudly to me. She kissed me on the cheek. "I know how to save you," she whispered before she drew away.

I stood wondering how she could save us, or even if she knew what she was talking about.

"Always getting kissed by natives," muttered Dana.

"What did she tell you?" whispered Paul quickly.

"No more talking please," admonished a guard.

"Hope," I whispered to Paul. I knew he'd figure out what that meant.

We were gathered and sat down, still tied up, in the middle of town where guards could watch us. We were allowed to speak to each other.

"What are we going to do?" asked Gale immediately.

"I have no idea," sighed Grant. "Obviously we're not going to kill each other."

"Is there any way to escape?" Vince said in a low voice.

"No," replied Grant. "I saw men in trees on our way into town. They're everywhere."

Everybody's voice was shaky. We were all scared, not that we shouldn't be allowed a little fear. Mostly it was emotions. We were all emphatically stating we were not going to kill each other. The very thought of it was revolting.

The only person not talking was Prof. Taylor, and that was worrying me. What was he going to do? I prayed he'd do nothing.

They made us stay in the center of their town, so they could watch us. That night, they made us lie down next to each other and go to sleep. I tried to fall asleep. I could hear some of the others snoring.

"Rick?" whispered Jane. She was right next to me.

"What?"

"I was just making sure you're okay."

"I'm fine." Not really a lie. "How are you?"

I heard her swallow. "I'm scared. I don't know what's going to happen. I don't want to see any of you guys die. It'd be...awful."

"I know, I know. Give me your hand." She put her hand in mine. Hers was cold. "I can't tell you not to be scared, because there's no way any of us can't be. But it's going to be okay. If we die, if they kill us, no matter how awful, as far as I can tell most of us are going to see each other soon after."

"You're right." Her answer gave me closure. "But, I wish we could get out of here."

I would have told her Chloe had a plan, but first of all I didn't know if the plan was any good, and secondly I wasn't close enough to her to whisper it. We were whispering already, and I knew the guard walking around us could hear what we were saying. "We'll be okay," I repeated, squeezing her hand.

"Thank you."

I didn't ask her what for. I fell asleep soon after.

Day Three Hundred Ninety Seven, the next day, we were awakened and lined up to take the hike up Mount Leopold.

"How big is it?" I asked Paul

"Dude." The way he said it, I knew it was big. "It's right in front of the village. I don't know how we're going to climb it. I don't know how we'll get Darby and Karen up there either, but the native dudes are picking up their stretchers like they're ready to go."

We walked uphill for a while, then stopped. "Dude," Paul said, leaning close to me, "they have an elevator."

My jaw fell open. "A *what?*"

"It's really big and, like, all ornate-looking. They're going to get us all in there, I guess. Uh-oh, here comes Ghost Girl."

"Rick!" Chloe called, coming up to me. "I have been granted my wish to show you my favor." She draped something around my neck. "It is the medallion of my ancestors. They will guide you." She got closer to me. "I have a plan."

A plan which she proceeded to tell me.

I never, ever would have given her credit for coming up with something that might work – yet her plan was plausible. Somewhere in her unassuming little head, she was a mastermind of tricks. Maybe it was her view on her faith that made her see this situation the way she did, which allowed her to come up with her plan to save us all. Maybe she wasn't a Nature believer in the way that the rest of the Naturalists were. Maybe it was just because she wanted us all to live.

Whatever the reason, I knew it was a good plan. I just had no idea whether it would work. It would all come down to my persuasion skills, which weren't too bad, but would need a little help from the Drama Department.

All these thoughts ran through my brain at lightening speed while the natives prepared us to get on the elevator.

"It is up to you now," said Chloe meaningfully. She went away.

Her mother, Helen, was with us. She was chanting some sort of blessing over us, which I wasn't too thrilled about. She stopped when she came to me. "Richard," she said, respect in her voice. "I am honored to see you again."

"Thanks," I said indifferently.

"You must be brave today."

"Yeah." *If only you knew what I was going to do. It was your daughter's idea, by the way.*

"May I say a blessing over you?"

"No."

"I see." She moved away. "Now, this Carrier will take you to the top of the mountain. As with most of our machines, it is run through channels to power stations at the waterfalls that surround us. When you are at that top, we will untie you, and your fight will begin."

My stomach clenched. This was it. I followed everyone into the elevator. It was a slow, shaky ride up. The natives were murmuring amongst themselves, and some of us were saying things to each other. I was standing next to Jane. I could smell Lilly of the Valley. I leaned closer to her. "Which one? I have to know."

"We are stopping now!" called Theodoric as the Carrier started to shake.

"Michael," Jane breathed before we were herded out of the elevator.

I was surprised. I would have bet she'd pick Colin. That choice seemed obvious. Then again, I understood why it was Grant. I was actually glad she picked him. Colin was great, but Grant and Jane just…went together.

"You will be positioned in a circle," called Theodoric. "The two sick will be positioned in the center."

We were being untied. I heard Chloe's voice behind me. "Ready?"

"Ready."

"I will count down to the beginning of the battle," continued Theodoric, "and then I and your guards will watch from the Carrier. When the battle is over, I will award the champion with my crown."

I breathed in.

"Ten…"

Chapter 20

It hit me like a tsunami. In nine seconds I was going to do something that would lead to my death, or I was going to save my own life along with the lives of my eleven friends. For one awful moment fear overwhelmed me. I felt hot and cold, sick, and frenzied at the same time.

"Seven…"

I breathed in again. I prayed: God save us.

"Five…four…three…two…one."

Everything went wrong.

Prof. Taylor shouted, "I am sorry to all of you that I had to do this – but it was the right thing to do. I took the handgun-" I heard a click "-not with the intention of killing you, but of letting you die. You are going to die for a cause, at least. These people, though you think they are occultists, are the most profoundly correct people I have ever encountered."

"Taylor, please," reasoned Grant calmly, "you don't have to do this. We'll admit you're our leader. We can end this without anyone getting hurt."

I backed slowly in the direction of the Carrier, taking slow, careful steps. *She said six steps back.*

"That's not the way it's supposed to go, Mr. Grant," responded Taylor. "You'll never truly submit to me or these people. They deserve a leader who is unhampered by the opinions of his former peers. You never listened to my opinions, not with heartfelt interest. These people will understand me."

"So you're going to shoot us, right here and now," said Colin. "Sure, Taylor. Look me in the eye and pull that trigger."

I paused.

"No!" shouted Jane. "Colin, you don't understand him!"

"She's right you know," said Taylor.

I heard the crack of a gunshot.

I tried to shut out any awful pictures in my mind and again took steps backward. ...*four, five...*

More gunshots, someone screaming, someone reasoning...

Six. I stepped back and felt the surface under me change from smooth to rocky. Chloe said the center of the mountain-top, called the Ring, had been smoothed out and painted for ceremonies. The ceremonies included death rituals, in which the Machine allowed the Ring to drop down a shaft under it to symbolize the fall of a spirit, or...something like that. The point was it dropped suddenly, deadly, almost to ground-level.

I was no longer standing on the Ring, but on the actual mountain rock. I reached behind me to feel a lever. I grasped it firmly. "Taylor!" I called, praying to God I was right about his character and he'd listen to me. "I'm afraid I've outsmarted all of you!"

"Ah!" said Taylor. I heard him come closer. "You? The little blind boy?"

"That's what you all think of me," I said through my teeth. I was really going to have to play this. "I'm always in the background, always quiet, always watching you – without seeing! Not with my eyes, but seeing with my mind. You never gave me respect, not the kind I deserved. I was always the little blind boy to you!" I spat. "Not any more!

Now I have all of your lives in my hand, one hand! That's all it takes to pull this lever."

"And what does that lever do?"

"You're standing on what the natives call the Ring. If I pull this lever, the Ring will drop to ground level, and all of you will die on impact."

"How do you know this?"

I grinned, hoping it looked evil. "I've been talking to the little native girl. None of you ever knew."

"You won't do it," Taylor stated.

"Yes. I will. You don't understand, Professor. You don't understand what I've been through. My family and friends are all dead. I can't see any more, and I was trapped on this stupid island for a very, very long time. And in all that time, after all I have been through, I was nothing to you!" I paused a moment, hoping it was effective, and realizing what I was saying was entirely untrue. I had never felt more special than I did when I was around these people, the people Taylor was killing, my friends. "Now, it's different."

"My God," Taylor whispered. "You would do it." His voice changed. "What if I shoot you first?"

"I can still pull the lever, and I will still have killed all of you. I will still be the champion. You can't deny that, Taylor. You thought you'd go behind our backs, and I did this right in front of you, all of you! That toast I gave to all of you? It was a lie. I despise all of you. Now I've won. Think of the proverb, Taylor. We've fought to the death. I've already won. No matter what you do, I'll end up killing you."

He sighed. "Yes, you've won. I cannot believe it. This whole time I thought I was the destined leader of these people. How could I not see it?" I heard a clatter, and knew he'd dropped the gun. "Theodoric!" he called. "You have your champion!"

I heard the natives come out of the elevator. "It is extraordinary!" Theodoric marveled. "One of your weakest is now our leader."

"Where is the gun?" I asked.

"Here." Chloe came and put it in my hands. "You did it," she whispered happily.

"Is anyone dead?" I said quietly.

"We're not yet sure," she answered

"Please help the ones he shot. I don't want anyone to die."

"I know. I'll tell the guards." She went away.

"Theodoric?" I said, trying to sound authoritative, "I want Prof. Taylor tied up. I'm sorry Taylor, but you brought mistrust on yourself."

"I know," he said ashamedly. "And you will never untie me, will you, Rick? You'll never trust me. So-" I heard footsteps, like he was running away. Then the noise stopped.

"He jumped off the edge of the mountain," said Theodoric incredulously.

I shook my head. "Too bad. Maybe he could have changed."

"Your value of life is inspirational," Theodoric said. "Your goal was to save your comrades all along, was it not?"

"Yes. How many of them are hurt?"

"The doctor, I fear, will not make it," he said sadly.

I bit my lip. God, save them.

Theodoric continued. "Your leader was shielding the woman who called to the doctor. Your leader was shot, and I think the woman was as well. And a young man and woman who were standing together may have been injured. The very tall man and the dark-haired woman are all right. But the two that were sick – I think the young man was protecting the woman, and they were both shot. I do believe they are dead. There is a man who is by the sick woman's body, crying."

Darby was protecting Karen? Poor guy. We always misjudged him. "We've got to save as many as we can."

"My people are trying to save them, my leader. May I place my crown on your head? It is a very simple crown, but I was a simple leader."

I stood there, trying to get my mind to stop whirling around. It just hit me that I had done it, I'd stopped the killing. And I was the leader now. That was going to be interesting. "Sure," I said.

He set it on my head. I reached up to feel it. It was a simple twisted ring of metal. "How did you do it?" he asked.

"Win? Oh. Taylor thought to win he actually had to kill us, physically. But I won anyway, by battling with the mind." I tapped my head, hoping to sound more intellectual than confused. "Anyway…I owe it to your daughter. If it weren't for her, my friends and I would be dead."

"She is a very good daughter," he said proudly. "You have shown me something, my leader – a new way to look at things. I always believed that the only way for our new leader to win was to eliminate his competition. I would have fought to kill if I were in such a position. But you were able to win and at the same time save your people."

"I hope I was," I sighed.

"Helen is highly educated in medicine, as is Chloe."

"Hmm." I was picturing those two chanting and waving Magic Dust around.

"You seem unconvinced of their abilities. Yes, they will pray, but they use physical medicine as well."

I figured these people were smart enough to do that. "Can you please take me to where our doctor is?"

"Of course." He led me over to Colin, and I sat down.

Helen and Jane were there. Jane was crying. I didn't blame her. My eyes started to water. "How is he?" I asked, my voice shaky.

"Hey, it's Wonder Boy," Colin murmured. "You did it."

I bit my lip hard. "I didn't do anything important. Just the right thing."

"I didn't figure he'd shoot, you know." His voice was strained. "Got his attention off Grant, though. Is Grant okay?"

"He is also very hurt," answered Helen. "But he will make it, I think."

"Lucky devil," Colin muttered characteristically. "Hey, Rick, c'mere."

"What?" I leaned close to him.

"Make sure he takes care of Jane."

"Colin, don't go," I begged.

"Can't help it. But I'll see you later."

"Colin, I'm sorry-" broke in Jane.

"No, none o' this mushy stuff. No drama. I'm okay."

I heard Jane get up and walk away.

Colin didn't say anything after that.

"He's gone," said Helen.

I rubbed my face and squeezed my eyes shut, trying not to let tears come out.

"Come," Helen said, taking my arm. "You must say good-bye to the sick boy."

"Oh, no," I breathed. We went to Darby. I could hear Zach crying softly nearby. Darby's breathing was shaky.

"There is nothing I can do here," Helen told me. "The bleeding is too great. And he was too weak already."

"Darby? If you can hear me, squeeze my hand." I held his hand. His grasped mine and then went limp again. "I'm sorry for every bad thing I ever said to or about you. We will miss you, we can't deny that. I wish this hadn't happened."

"He, too, is dead now," Helen said after a few moments. "But he was smiling."

"Zach?" I called.

"I'll be okay," he said bravely.

"Are you hurt?" Helen asked him.

"No. No, he just shot her."

"Zach-" I began.

"It's okay."

I nodded. Zach seemed like a sturdy guy.

"Rick!" I was so relieved to hear Paul's voice. He came up to me and put a hand on my shoulder. "Rick, I can't believe it."

"I'm here, too," said Dana helpfully.

"Are you guys okay?"

"Nothing I cannot cure," said Helen. "Your former leader is behind you. Chloe is tending to him, and a tall man and a dark-haired woman are with him."

"Thanks." I went on my hands and knees over to Grant.

"Rick," Chloe greeted me.

"How is he?"

She hesitated. "He has a better chance than the doctor."

"Which isn't much," said Grant.

"You'll make it," I told him, sounding confident. "Colin said you had to take care of Jane."

"What? Guess I'll have to make it, then..."

"He's unconscious now," said Chloe. "Please, hand me that piece of cloth there."

"You guys alright?" I asked Gale and Vincent.

"Not a scratch," answered Vince.

"Go talk to Jane," said Gale in a motherly way. She turned me around. "She's straight that way."

I stayed on my hands and knees, regardless of whether that looked silly. I didn't have my walking stick and I didn't feel like taking any chances of falling off the mountain. I heard Jane crying and went and sat next to her. "Grant's gonna make it," I told her.

She sniffed. "Oh, Rick, why did he kill Colin?"

"You loved him more than you thought?"

"I did love him, like I loved everybody. It isn't that, its just – he was a good man. It shouldn't have happened to him." She breathed in thickly. "I shouldn't be crying like this."

"Why not? Colin deserved mourning."

"I keep praying to God Michael won't die."

I found it moving that she was calling Grant by his first name. "I always thought Michael was a nice name..." I mused out loud.

She made a funny noise, like a laugh. "Oh, ow."

"Are you hurt?" I asked, suddenly alarmed.

"It's just my arm."

"'Just your arm?' That's an important limb, woman! Go see Helen."

"She's busy," Jane argued quietly.

"Look, I worked pretty hard to rescue you. Don't you go bleeding to death."

"Rick, you are so funny." She patted my shoulder, got up and left.

I took in a big breath and let it all out very slowly. What was I going to do now? I was supposed to be some kind of leader to these people, and I had no clue what I was going to do. The first thing was, I'd have to be confident in myself before they believed I could do anything. I was always pretty confident I could do things, so that might not be too hard.

Secondly, I was going to figure out a way to use their technology to build a radio. Then we'd contact help and get off this island. We could live with the natives for a while. There was a hope, I thought, of their reforming from their religion, but we still needed to get out of here.

I sat there for quite a while, when someone came up behind me. "We're going back down to the village now," said Chloe. "They've taken the bodies already. Now everyone's in the Carrier waiting for us."

"Grant?" I asked tiredly.

"He will be fine." She sounded like she was smiling. I wasn't sure she fully grasped that she'd saved our lives.

"I owe you for everything. We all owe you. Why exactly did you help me?"

She took my hand and guided me towards the Carrier. "I don't think you were meant to die."

"What does that mean, Chloe?"

"It means...there must have been some other plan intended. I don't think the way to resolve things is to kill."

"It's a good thing you're so tender-hearted. And intelligent." I mumbled her words, "Another plan." So God had had a plan all along...

"You think I'm intelligent?" she asked shyly.

"Totally." *A little weird, but intelligent.* We got in the elevator.

"Flirt," whispered Dana, poking me.

I shook my head and smiled. We were all going to be okay.

Chapter 21

Five months later.
A swarm of reporters were all lined up outside the L.A. hotel, demanding that they needed to speak to a certain group of guests inside, whom they referred to as 'The Survivors.' They were not allowed in. They were told, very politely, that the survivors needed absolute quiet. The reporters didn't seem to be listening.

The renowned survivors themselves were on the fourth floor, in separate rooms, trying without much success to get some sleep.

It had been a long week, ever since we contacted a ship using a make-shift radio. The ship had contacted the American government, who'd sent three rescue planes to pick up the eight survivors of lost Flight 344. We were flown to a military base, then to L.A., where they checked us in at a comfortable hotel to get some rest. In a few days there would be dozens of interviews to attend to, talk-shows to be on, and then, when all that died down, we could go back to our normal lives.

At the moment, the only thing we wanted was soft beds, hamburgers, and cable TV.

The Survivors had agreed to an interview with a reporter named Kent White. The reason Mr. White got an interview was because he was a man who was known to tell an entire story, entirely truthfully, whether that made him unpopular in the media or not. Not to mention the fact that he, too, had been involved in an airplane crash that killed his wife. It was that point of sympathy that had won him the interview.

Mr. White was a quiet man, very polite, casual and understanding. He had contacted the survivors personally, and when they said "No interview," he didn't call again.

Eventually, after continual media harassment, The Survivors decided on one thing - they would all tell the story to one reporter, and they decided on Kent White. They called him back. He was to talk to them one at a time, one day at a time. He agreed.

Mr. White was now in room four-two-nine, talking with his first interviewee, Mr. Rick Ferrell.

The interview went like this: Rick talked while Mr. White recorded the conversation, listening intently.

Mr. White found Rick an interesting young man, to say the least. He sat in the round hotel chair, knees drawn up to his chest, head tilted to the side. He wore a t-shirt and jeans, both of which were worn and a little loose, and he went barefoot. It seemed he hadn't had to time to shop for new clothes or re-adjust to civilization. Maybe he didn't want to.

After quite some time, the interview came to a close.

"Thank you very much, Rick." Mr. White smiled warmly. "May I ask you a few more questions?"

"Sure."

"What was the saddest past of this experience?"

Rick took a moment to think. "The saddest was when I found out Noah had died."

"What was the happiest moment?"

Rick rubbed the back of his neck. "Well...it wasn't one moment. After I went berserk on Jane, I felt a kind of release. Afterwards, I felt better about things. I didn't feel...stuck any more."

"After you're done touring the country, appearing on talk-shows – what will you do?"

"Good question. Mom had a friend named Sharon who lives in Texas. When she heard I was alive she called me and said she'd take me in. She and her husband are really nice. I see them every Christmas. Well, except for last Christmas, of course."

"You're very young, to have experienced all of this. What got you though?"

"My faith in Jesus Christ," he replied firmly. "No matter what happened, I knew he was allowing things for a reason. He had some kind of plan."

"Amazing." Mr. White stood up. "Oh, one more thing; did any of the natives – Naturalists-" he smiled "-ever change from their beliefs?"

"Some, a little. But I don't give up hope. The natives said we can come back and visit. I don't know if I could. They don't understand how I feel about them or that island. It wouldn't be a pleasure visit for me, but if I did go back at all, it'd be to see Chloe. She's different from them. I'd like to get her out of there." Standing there, saying that, he didn't seem like a fifteen-year-old. He seemed much older.

"Here." Mr. White handed him a map. "They sent copters over the island to map it. I got one with raised lines."

"It's not in Braille, is it?" Rick asked suspiciously.

"No."

He ran a hand over the map. "Huh. The island is shaped like a cross. Like a grave-marker," he added solemnly. "Did they ever name it?"

"No, actually. There is no record of it ever having been discovered or claimed before this. It doesn't have a name yet. What would you call it?"

"I'm not sure."

"Usually the name describes the place," Mr. White said helpfully.

Rick lifted his head. His unseeing eyes lowered, he whispered, "Black."

Printed in the United States
86968LV00002B/86/A

9 781602 668324